Paradox Of Time & Choice

RB Parkline

Published by RB Parkline, 2024.

This is a work of fiction. Similarities to real people, places, or events are entirely coincidental.

PARADOX OF TIME & CHOICE

First edition. March 7, 2024.

Copyright © 2024 RB Parkline.

ISBN: 979-8224109142

Written by RB Parkline.

Chapter I

The only thing Ela could do was run. She dropped everything and ran for the limestone outcropping. She had seen the big cat lurking in the high grass knowing it was stalking her. Ela knew her chance of escaping the huge powerful tiger was none. She had to try so she ran. Reaching the wall of stone she did not look back knowing the tiger would be close. It didn't matter she knew the tiger was fast and would be running at full speed in a few leaps. She crawled up the rock quickly and, searching desperately, spotted a small ledge overhang. She raced up the rock, her fingers desperately grabbing the loose soft rock as she climbed knowing her life was hanging in the balance.

The big cat was silent but Ela knew he had to be close. She stepped onto the narrow ledge and carefully moved onto it her heart was beating hard from the run as well as the fear that gripped her. She glanced down and saw she was high on the rockface. She was not sure if the narrow ledge would hold her weight. It didn't matter, she thought to herself. If the big cat caught her she was dead. If she fell she hoped she would be killed immediately not wanting to die from the powerful bite from the large teeth of the tiger.

Her small feet were barley on the ledge as she moved across it. She turned seeing the big cat looking at her with large yellow eyes. The hate and anger was obvious as he saw the easy prey moving away from him. The tiger with a large paw on the ledge raised his other paw with long sharp claws extended taking a swipe at her. The claws missed her by mere inches. The powerful claws dung into the limestone creating deep gashes. The tiger screamed in frustration. Ela moved away even though the ledge was becoming more narrow.

The tiger was testing the ledge as it looked down seeing the distance was a long way down. He looked at the small woman on the ledge and moved his paw on the ledge closer to her. Suddenly the big cat screamed in pain as it lost its footing and tumbled down the rockface. Ella looked down at the cat seeing it had hit the ground hard.

The large tiger stood up and screamed so loud it scared Ela who stood on the narrow ledge, her fingers digging into the rock. She saw the tiger stagger then watched as it started with a limp running toward a man that was standing holding a strange stick that was bowed.

Ela's eyes narrowed as she looked at the man who was strange. She did not recognize him. She was surprised as she realized he was tall and had no hair on his face. She watched in shock and fear as the tiger was running directly at the man. He did not move. Her eyes narrowed seeing the man reach into the strange pack on his back. He removed a long slender spear, placed it on the long stick and pulled the string back and when he released it the small spear flew at a tremendous speed hitting the tiger in the chest. The tiger rolled over head first. The tiger stood up screaming. The strange tall man removed another small spear and placed it on the stick. Pulling back the string the man released it striking the tiger in the neck. The tiger went down. The man walked toward the beast keeping a safe distance from it, carrying a heavy club. He approached as the tiger growled low, turning and watching the man approach him from behind. The man raised the club and struck the tiger twice on the head. The tiger lay quiet as the man walked up removing a knife and stuck it in the tigers throat.

Ela hanging on the rock face watched in fascination. No one in her tribe had ever killed a big tiger. She was shocked. She slowly began to make her way carefully across the narrow ledge. She stepped onto the solid rock staring in disbelief as the strange man began to skin the big cat.

Stepping down from the rock Ela stood watching the man working to remove the skin from the large tiger. She hesitantly walked toward the man. She stopped and picked up her bag made from beaver skin along with her digging stick. The man did not look up as he concentrated on his work. He pulled the skin back and using a sharp knife slowly removed the tough hide. It was hot and the work was tedious.

He looked over his shoulder seeing the girl standing watching him. She was the first human he had seen since he had arrived. He turned to look at the girl. He thought to himself she was not the young girl he had first thought. She was a woman. A small woman, he guessed she was close to four and a half feet tall. She had a nice looking face with long black hair that looked as if it hadn't been combed, black eyes with dark skin. She had a slightly protruding brow. Her jaw was thick with a small chin. He turned his attention to the big cat he was skinning.

The man had the skin off one side. He stood up to turn the tiger over on its other side. He saw the woman was closer. She was watching him intently. When he finished removing the skin from the large tiger, he sat back tired from the work. He watched the woman walk over, grasping the hide and pulling on it, stretching it out on the ground. She removed a small stone knife and began cleaning the skin of meat and blood.

The tall man walked to the cat, took out a small hatchet and began hitting the top of the cat's head. When the head split open he pulled it open and removed the brain, taking it to the hide dropping it on the skin. The woman cut the brain into pieces and began to smear it on the skin.

The man helped her work the brain matter into the pelt. The woman stood up walking to the tiger removing the claws from the huge tiger with her stone knife. The man sat watching her. She looked at him and pointed to the head saying something he did not understand. She spoke in a low tone moving her hands rapidly as she spoke. The man sat not understanding her. She walked to the tiger's head pointing to the large protruding tusks extending from the cat's mouth. The man sighed, standing up and walked to the tiger. Removing his knife he began to cut the large tusks that were pointing down out of the tiger's mouth. It took him some time to remove the two tusks. He stood up after he was done seeing the woman standing looking at him. She had rolled the hide up and had it tied to her back. He walked to her, handing her the two large tusks. She placed them in her large bag hanging from a strap on her shoulder.

It didn't seem right having the woman carry the hide but he thought she was no doubt grateful for being saved from being eaten. They walked for some time toward a large forest. He stopped at a stream and dropped his bag along with the bow and arrows he carried on his back. He removed his shirt. He looked at the woman as his face went slightly red, he dropped his pants walking into the water. It was hot and he wanted to cool off as well as take a bath.

Ela stood quietly watching the man. She had never seen a person go into the water. She was surprised to see the man who had brown arms was white where the shirt and pants covered him. She sat the pelt down with her bag and walked to the water washing her face and neck. She cupped her hands and drank the clear water. She sat back watching the man swim in the water. She was not sure what to think of the strange man. He was taller than anyone she had ever met. He did not have hair on his face and his hair was not long. It was also light colored. His eyes were also light color. They were the color of the spring grass.

The man came out of the water after a while and dressed. He sat next to Ela and said something in a strange language. She did not understand him. He stood up picking up his bow and arrows. He picked up the skin and began walking toward the trees. Ela was not sure what to do. She knew her people were probably at the cave by now. She knew it was in the direction of the rising sun. it would be a long journey and she would not be there before it was dark. She did not want to spend the night on the open ground alone. She watched the man who stopped and turned around looking at her. She followed him.

Ela was surprised as the man walked into the trees. She was afraid of the forest knowing wild beasts lived in the trees. She cautiously followed the tall man. The forest was dark with the trees blocking the sun. Soon she was in an open area in the trees.

The man walked to a tree and sat the tiger's hide down as well as his arrows on his back. He sat the end of the bow on the ground and pushed the other end down removing the string. Ella was fascinated watching the man. He removed the black knife that looked strange to Ella. He picked up several long strands of leather strips and with his knife made small holes in the hide. She watched the man lace the thin strips of leather through the holes in the hide, then tied the strips onto the trees stretching the tiger's pelt tight. In her mind she had done this many times in the past, but not with a tiger pelt.

When he finished he walked to a tree. Ela looked seeing there was some kind of shelter in the tree. She watched the man climb up pieces of limbs that were tied to the tree. He disappeared into the structure. Ela was surprised as part of the structure was removed and an opening appeared. She saw the man inside the strange structure motioning for her to come to him. She walked to the tree seeing the limbs tied to the tree. Ela was not sure what to do. She wanted the safety of the cave. This did not seem safe. She looked up seeing the man looking down at her. Ela did not want to spend the night outside so she slowly began climbing up.

Inside the structure was a solid floor of tree branches. There was meat hanging from the top of the ceiling. She watched the man go to a hearth of stones. Her sharp eyes saw as he removed a stone from a pouch he wore on his waist, then began striking it with another stone. She watched sparks coming from the stone, soon she saw the man lean over blowing on the hearth. She saw the familiar sight of fire.

Ela stepped back in fear. Her back was against the wall. She could not believe the man had started the fire with stones. He must be a shaman, he had power, magic, perhaps he was a spirit. She reached into her pack removing the small stone that was shaped like a woman with a large belly. She grasped it tightly and asked the Mother to protect her.

The man saw her and continued to add sticks to the fire. He knew she was afraid. He went to the rear of the structure where meat was hanging and removed a large rabbit. He placed it over the fire on a stick suspended on two other sticks. He sat quietly watching the woman as she had her head down. He turned the rabbit as the smell of cooking meat filled the house in the trees.

When the rabbit was done he removed it, cutting off the legs with the thighs. He placed two legs on a plate that was woven from reeds. He said "dinners ready."

The woman looked up. He pointed to the plate of food. Ela watched him go to a container and pour out water in a strange small container. He sat it down and pointed to her then to the food.

Ela walked to the food and sat down. The fire was burning brightly. She saw the man eating the cooked rabbit. She thought the man could not be a spirit. She began eating and realized how hungry she was. The food was good.

As she ate she studied the strange flat plate. She knew it was from the reeds in the water. She was intrigued as it had been woven tightly together to form a flat plate. She looked seeing other strange woven objects sitting around the structure as well as stone looking containers. She realized they were not stone, they were similar but different.

Finishing the meal the two sat and looked at each other. The man was five foot ten and had a different look from the small dark woman. He pointed to a long bed that was laying next to the window. The woman looked surprised as she stood up going to the bed. The man stood up walking to the window, pulling it shut. He secured it then went to the opening where the ladder was located and placed a wooden cover over the opening. He secured it with leather straps. He walked to the bed and was surprised to see the woman on her hands and knees with her head down. He was not sure what she was doing;

Ela had interpreted the man wanting her to go to his bed meant he wanted to mate with her. She had been given to a man of her tribe as his mate. He had left her after being together for two years. She did not give him a child so he chose to go to another tribe where he became the leader after a year. Ela lay quiet on her knees and hands with her head down. She felt his hand on her small wrist. She looked up as the man was looking at her. He helped her up. She was being rejected. She felt humiliated knowing no man wanted her since her mate had left her not giving him children.

The man walked with her to the back of the room. He poured water into a bowl picking up a soft yellow ball . It was soap he had made from wood ashes and animal fat. Using a soft deer skin he dipped it into the water, rubbed the deer skin over the yellow ball and gently washed her face. Ela was not sure what to think. The man knew the young woman was dirty, and had a strong odor. He washed the dirt and sweat from her face, neck and arms. He removed her shirt and began washing her back, chest, and stomach. The man knew she was a woman seeing the small full breasts. He removed her pants and washed her legs. He poured the water onto her hair and began to rub it together with pieces of the yellow ball. The man poured fresh water over body including her hair. He dried her off with soft fur. He ran his fingers through her hair removing most of the tangles.

Ella stood quiet as he began to braid her hair. When he finished he tied the end with a thin piece of hide. She had never had anyone pay so much attention to her. She looked at her hair that was braided and thought how it looked good to her. Ella looked up at the man curiously. He smiled at her. He seemed so odd.

The man taking her hand walked with her to the bed and helped her lay down. Ela watched him pour out the water and pour in freshwater. He undressed and began cleaning himself. He walked to the bed and laid down. She was surprised as he pressed his lips against hers. It was an odd feeling. She had not had anyone do this before. She felt his hand touching her. The man made love to her.

Chapter II

Ela woke up hearing thunder and the crack of lightning. She looked around realizing she was in the strange structure in the trees. She saw the man laying next to her. He was so odd. His ways were different from anything she had seen, or heard of. She rose, reaching for her clothes. She looked at the hair he had woven together and she liked it. Dressing in the dim light she looked at him wondering where this strange man came from. He was strange but she thought he was strong and nice looking.

She went to the hearth and stirring the coals started a fire. Going to her bag she removed tea leaves and a small stone pot she would use to heat water. She found water in a strange looking container she had thought was rock. It appeared to be made from dried mud. It held water which impressed her. She looked at the strange small spears thinking they were so small and nothing like the heavy spears the men of her tribe used. She saw the man was awake watching her. She was embarrassed and walked back to the fire. She put mint leaves in the water and sat with her head down.

The man stood up and dressed. He walked to the arrows, taking one he brought it to the woman. She looked at him as he handed it to her. She reached up, taking the arrow. It was so strange looking. There were feathers on one end with a strange small sharp point on the other end. The man handed her his knife. She studied it as he sat down. The blade was smooth and black. She ran her small thumb over the edge and was surprised at how sharp it was. She looked at the man who was watching her. The man rose and walked to a basket that was made from woven reeds. He removed some powder, placed it in a bowl, pouring water on it. He worked it with his hands until he had a small round cake. He made several of the cakes. Ela watched the man take fat and put it on a thin stone he placed over the fire. She handed him a small wooden cup with weak tea. She watched as the fat became liquid. The man spread it over the thin rock then placed the cakes on the rock.

The man walked to the wall next to his bed and united the leather strips then pushed the wood sliding it so the opening allowed light in. Ela walked to the opening and looked outside. It was raining hard. She was surprised to see no rain was coming in the shelter. She had stayed in shelters on long hunts. They were nothing like this. Standing near the man she felt his hand on her shoulder. She looked up at him. He leaned over placing his lips on hers. She thought it was strange. She looked out the window and saw the trees and the sky with the falling rain. She did not know what to think.

They walked back to the fire where the man with a flat stick flipped the cakes over. They were brown on one side. After a short while the man placed two cakes on the flat woven plate and handed it to her. She watched the man pick one up and eat it. Ela hesitantly took a bite. It was something she had not tasted before. It was good.

They finished eating breakfast. Ela patted her chest, "Ela." the man sat quiet then said "Ela"

She pointed to him. He sat quietly. He did not know his name. He was not aware of how he arrived in this strange place. He had woken up naked in tall grass. He had made a bow with arrows and built the tree house. He had begun hunting for food. She was the first person he had seen in almost six months. He looked around the room seeing the talons from the eagle he had killed. He said "Talon."

Ela looked at him curiously. He pointed to the talons on the wall. She nodded as she recognized them. "Talon." she said in her low voice.

They would sit in the treehouse and talk with Ella teaching him her language. He caught on quickly. It rained all day so they did not leave.

The following morning Ella followed Talon out of the tree house. He showed her how he strung the bow. She watched as he shot arrows at a soft embankment which was far off. She followed him to the river where he walked in and picked up a strange cone shaped object that appeared to be made from sticks woven together. Two fish were inside. She was surprised to see he had trapped fish. She followed him up the river checking several other traps. They were able to bring in eight large fish.

The fish were cleaned at the river and brought back to the treehouse. They spent the day smoking the fish. Later they walked out onto the open plains and soon saw several large rabbits. Talon with his bow brought down two of them. They were cleaned and the pelts were stretched tight to cure in the sun.

The following morning Ela explained she needed to return to her cave and her people. She asked Talon to go with her. He did not want her to go, and he did not want to leave his treehouse. He was not sure of the people in her tribe. He enjoyed having the woman with him and she was a great help with the animals and fish he caught.

Ela was determined to return to her cave with her people. They left the house in the trees early in the morning. Talon walked with her for most of the day heading east. He was able to kill a young antelope. When it was skinned he placed the meat inside the skin giving it to her.

She was able to tell him her cave was not far. He leaned over with his hand on her face. He looked intently into her dark eyes. Leaning down he pressed his lips on hers. He watched her walk away.

A young woman stopped her work, scraping a hide from a buffalo. She saw Ela walking toward the camp in the fading light. She was surprised to see Ela. She had heard how Ela had been separated from the rest of the hunters and women with them. She stood up slowly and walked toward the camp then began running. She told a group of women she had seen Ela's spirit coming. The women were alarmed as many of them ran for the cave. Ana, who was Ela's friend, walked to the edge of the camp. Ela smiled and walked toward her. She hugged Ana. "Are you a spirit?" Ana asked breathlessly.

"No, Ana I am alive as you are. I have a story to tell."

Ana smiled, "I would think so Ela. you have been gone for four days." Ana's eyes narrowed as she looked at Ela. "You have woven your hair, it looks strange."

The men and women of the cave gathered around Ela as she sat the heavy skin with meat down. It was getting dark and all were anxious to be inside the cave. A heavy skin was placed over the opening of the cave to keep out any predators. The hearth fires were lit as families gathered around for their evening meal. Ela sat with Ana and her mate Boun with their two sons and a daughter. They ate in silence, each anxious to know what Ela had to say. They would wait for the evening when the tribe gathered in the center of the cave as a community. There they talked of events of the day or planned for the future. They often told stories for entertainment. They all knew it was more polite to wait for Ella to tell the whole tribe rather than answering many questions from individuals having to repeat herself.

The tribe gathered together in the center of the large cave. Ela stood near the fire and began to tell of how she was collecting mushrooms and digging roots. She realized the rest of the tribe had moved on. She walked for several miles when she saw a large cat stalking her. She reached in her bag and removed the two large tusks. The rest of the tribe gasped. She told of running for a large rock cliff and how the tiger was almost to catch her. She moved out on a small ledge. The tiger with a mighty swipe of his big claw was close to her. The tiger had missed her by inches. She took out the claws of the tiger holding them for the tribe to see. The tribe was stunned. She told of how a strange man holding a stick with a string on it, and a small spear killed the tiger. Ella explained the strange man was tall. She raised both arms up in the air and standing on her tiptoes told how she could not touch the top of the man's head if I reached this high, since he was so tall. The tribe sat quiet trying to understand Ela. They had never seen anyone so tall. She continued her tale explaining she followed the man staying with him in a structure in a tree. Ela explained how the man had used ash from the fire mixing with water and washing her body and hair, then weaving it. How he started a fire with two rocks. The strange man was able to catch fish in a trap. When she finished telling her story the tribe of men and women sat quietly all were shocked by Ella's story. No one had ever heard such a story.

Halmak a man from the tribe stood up saying "it is not our way to tell a story that is not true. You have brought shame on yourself by telling this story that is not true."

"It is true," Ela protested. "The man was tall and had skin that was white not dark. His hair was light and had no hair on his face. He was tall."

"It is not true!" Halmak yelled.

Dalk the leader sat quietly then said "Enough, how is it Ela survived alone for many days? She has the tusks of the great cat."

Halmak sat down "She is not truthful," He protested.

Dalk stood up helping his mate stand up. "Then we will go and see this strange man that can kill a great cat with tusks." He looked at the men sitting around. "How many of you have killed a great cat?" No one spoke. He looked at Ela "we will go see this tall man that starts a fire with two rocks."

Chapter III

It was dark when they left the cave. Dalk leading the way with Ela walking close beside him. Ela was afraid of the dark knowing many predators hunted in the dark. She walked close to Dalk with the ten other hunters also close. There was always safety in numbers. However, if a large predator was hungry they could be attacked. Ela was anxious to find Talon and show the others she was telling the truth. Halmak was a good hunter but he was stern and did not allow for any untruthfulness. He would correct any hunter that told a story and made it more exciting than it was. Being honest was important for all the tribe. A person who could not tell the truth could not be counted on. Halmak had shamed Ela by not believing her story. She knew it was a story that she would have not believed had she not been there.

The sun was hot as it rose. By midday the group stopped to rest and eat. Soon they were on their way. They arrived at the edge of the forest by early evening. The men hesitated as Ela walked into the forest. They followed her, each of them prepared for an attack. They were surprised when they came to a clearing and Ela pointed to the structure in the trees. Dalk walked slowly seeing the pelt of the tiger stretched between two trees. He looked at Halmak and said nothing. Ela climbed up the tree and looked inside the house. She climbed down saying "Talon is not here he may be checking the fish traps."

The group sat down each looking at the house then to the hides drying in the sun. They all stood up as a tall man walked into the clearing. He was tall. Dalk was five feet two and considered tall. This man was taller than any man they had ever seen, and he did not have hair on his face.

Talon stopped when he saw the men. He sat the small pig down he had killed and grasped his bow. He relaxed when he saw Ela walk to him. "Talon, I have come with men from my tribe."

He didn't quite understand everything she said but knew she had come with men. Dalk with the men following walked up to him. His large heavy spear with the heavy stone arrow head was pointing down. Talon knew he could no doubt use it effectively if needed. He listened as the man spoke. He did not understand him. Ela pointed to the arrows in his pack. He reached up, removing one handing it to Dalk.

Dalk studied the arrow as the other men looked at it. The arrow was small and slender, it did not seem heavy enough to kill a beast. Certainly not a big cat. He looked at Ela then to Talon. Talon showed Dalk the bow he took the arrow and showed how he placed the arrow with the notch in the end on the string. He slowly pulled the arrow back and released it. The arrow flew rapidly in the air striking the tiger pelt going through it. The men were shocked.

Ela picked up the pig and took it to the tree with the house and began cleaning it. She looked up saying "Talon your knife."

Talon handed her his knife. She showed it to Dalk and the men then began taking the tough skin of the pig off with the sharp knife. They were amazed. Dalk squatted down taking the knife. Holding the skin he removed it quickly with the sharp knife. He was amazed. He looked at the men. "I have never held such a knife. It may be magic." he looked at Ela, "how did he make this?"

Ela spoke to Talon who understood what Dalk was asking. "I will show you tomorrow." He reached in his pack and took out his hatchet that was made of the same material. The men inspected it and were impressed.

The men went into the tree house and again were impressed. It had never occurred to them to build a house in a tree. They believed a cave was the only safe place. However, being high away from predators did make sense. They all inspected the pottery and the woven baskets. They sat in the clearing as Ela prepared the meal. It was difficult to communicate but they were able to understand with hand gestures.

That evening as the sun sat Talon started a fire with two rocks. The men were shocked. They whispered in urgent voices how it must be magic. They ate the pig Talon had killed when it was cooked over the fire he had started. None of them knew for sure what to think. They had all heard Ela tell of this strange man, but to see him was something else. Was he a shaman with special power, or a spirit? They sat quietly for a while when Dalk told Ela he wanted Talon to come to the cave. Winter was coming and it would be safer for him in the cave during the cold season. Also he wanted Talon to hunt with him so he could see how the small spears worked.

Talon was hesitant, not sure he trusted the men. Dalk, who was impatient, stood up taking Talon's hand and Ela's small hand he put them together saying they were now mates. Talon understood and agreed to go with the men since he was concerned with spending the winter alone. He also missed Ela and wanted to be close to her. They stayed the night in the treehouse. It was a strange experience for the men.

They left the following day before the sun had come up. The pottery and woven baskets were taken. Talon walked to the creek and removed the traps. The men were amazed to see fish in the traps. The men carried the traps as they walked silently most of the day. After a long walk as the sun was sitting Talon saw in the distance a large cave. When they arrived the tribe was not sure what to think of Talon. He was tall and it was strange seeing a man with no hair on his face. He was also fair skinned.

The following days Talon showed the tribe how to weave baskets and make pottery for storing their supplies. Men followed Talon to an outcropping they had seen many times before. Talon instructed the men how he broke the rock that was black and also brittle. The volcanic rock that had been heated at such a high temperature from a volcano eruption was like glass. The rock was hard to work but the pieces were sharp. When the right sizes were obtained he showed them how he spit deer horn with the hatchet. With the two halves he placed one on each side of the sharp knife making a handle. He wrapped wet leather around the two pieces of horn so when it dried it shrank into place fitting tight. He also made several hatchets for the men. The small broken pieces he used to make the arrow heads he placed on the end of the arrows.

Talon taught the men to make a bow and how to use strong animal tendons to make sinew for the string. The arrows were cut and shaped from tree branches. Feathers from birds were also shaped and placed on the arrows with tree sap. The men soon were good marksmen with the bow and arrow.

In the evenings he stayed in the cave with Ela. She had begun washing herself and cleaning her hair. Ela taught the other women how to weave their hair. Many of the men also wanted their hair in a braid. They did not wash as often, although many of the tribe did wash more frequently.

Talon learned more of the tribe's language. The men went out hunting every day. Sometimes they were gone for days. They had to find enough meat to store up for the winter months. The back of the cave was cool and the smoked meat would be preserved there.

The men soon learned that the bow and arrows helped them tremendously. Talon and men would get close to a large deer and shoot it in the chest or neck which would slow it down. Men with heavy spears would rush in and finish it off. The pigs with tusks were dangerous and had hurt many hunters. The men with bow and arrows could slow the pig down enough for the men with spears to finish it off. The hunts were successful.

The women learned the techniques of weaving baskets and making pottery. Talon showed them where wild oats grew and they soon became a staple for the tribe, along with roots, berries and mushrooms. The oats when gathered and pounded into a fine powder would also keep well in woven baskets. With the fish traps women and children were bringing in fish. They were smoked like the other food so they would last throughout the cold season. The winter months would be long and hunting minimal. The tribe always suffered through the long cold months.

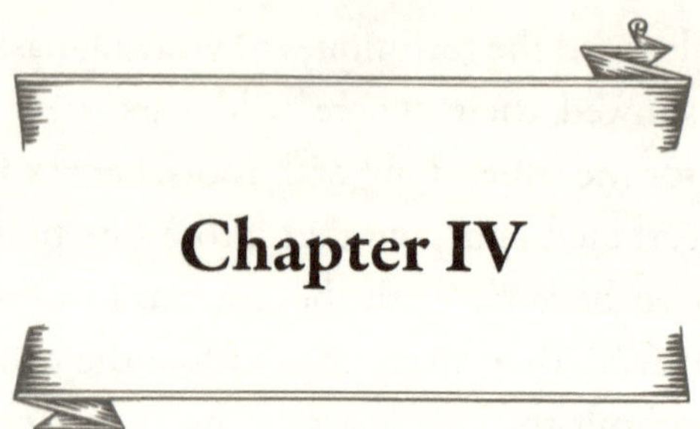

Chapter IV

The winter months were long and cold. Hunters would go out on a clear day. They often came back without food. Most of the animals had migrated and did not return until spring. A group of hunters had found a small herd of deer bringing in two. It was a time of celebration.

Each evening the tribe would gather around the large fire and listen to stories. It was entertaining and helped pass the long hours of winter nights. One evening Dalk said to Talon "you tell a story. We would like to know more of you and your people."

Talon was not sure what to say. He did not remember his past. He did not know of his people or how he came to be in the strange land. Somehow he did know how to survive. He was not even sure of how he knew the things he did know.

Talon stood up walking to the fire burning in the center of the cave. He looked at the people sitting and watching him. They were different from him. He cut his hair, keeping it short, and he removed the hair on his face with his sharp knife.

He sighed then began speaking. "Many years ago I was in a land far away. It was a cold winter and the snow fell hard for many days. I opened the door to my house, it was not a cave but a house in a tree. The snow had covered it up. All I could see was white snow. So I began eating the snow. I ate the snow all the way to the ground. Eating the snow I was able to make a path to the river. There I saw it was frozen over. It was so cold the birds were frozen in the sky. I threw a rock and knocked down a large fat goose. I carried the frozen goose back to my tree house following the trail I had cleared earlier. I started a fire in the hearth but it was so cold the fire froze. I broke off a piece of the fire with my hatchet and shoved the frozen fire up the goose's butt. The fire cooked the bird from the inside."

The tribe sat quietly, no one had ever heard such a wild tale. Halmak stood up slowly. "That is not true. You have shamed yourself by telling a story that is not true."

"How do you know it is not true?" Talon asked calmly.

Halmak yelled, "You did not eat snow to make a trail! No bird freezes in the air and fire does not freeze!" He was so angry he was shaking.

"Have you ever seen a bird frozen in the air?"

"No!" Halmak screamed.

"You did not believe Ela when she said I killed a big cat with the long tusks, or when she saw me start a fire with two rocks. Now all of you can start a fire with two rocks."

"Fire does not freeze. You can not cook a goose with frozen fire!"

"I was telling a jest. You see If I tell a story that is not true and expect you to believe it then that is not being honest. That is called a lie. However, if I tell you a story that is not true and do not expect you to believe it then that is a jest. I am only entertaining you. I do not expect you to believe the story." Talon said patiently.

"It is the same thing! You have told a story that is not true! You call it jest or what you want it is the same. It is not a true story." Halmak said angrily.

"It was a jest." Talon said, walking to where Ela sat.

Later that evening Ela stirred the coals lighting the fire. She put on a pot of water.

"Talon, you should not tell a story of jest. It is not right."

Talon smiled as he looked at Ela. "Did you like my story?"

She shook her head. "I did not understand it. It was not a true story."

Talon took her hand pulling her to him. She sat on his lap. She tried to get up but his strong arms were wrapped around her. "Not even a little bit?"

She looked at him, not understanding him. He often spoke so oddly. She tried to get up but he held her close. "The water is hot. I will fix you some tea."

He pressed his lips against hers. "You did like the story." He whispered in her ear.

He released her as she scrambled up quickly. She poured hot water into the small cup she had made that Talon had shown her how to mix clay from the river bank and dry it in the hot sun. "You should not tell a jest."

The following night the tribe sat quietly around the fire. No one had stood up to tell a story. The voices were low as people talked quietly. After a time Dalk said to Talon "You should tell a story."

Halmak spoke up quickly "no Dalk, He cannot tell a story that is true. He will say it is jest, but we know it is not a true story."

"I would like to hear Talon tell a story." Dalk said firmly.

Talon stood up "Many years ago I was hunting on a cold day. I saw a large herd of wooly mammoths. I knew I would not be able to kill one so I thought I would follow them and perhaps I would find something I could kill. Suddenly something spooked the mammoths and they started to run. They all turned and ran toward me. I started to run but they soon caught up with me. A large male stepped on me and since the ground was sandy it drove me straight down into the ground. I was driven far into the ground and soon found I was in a tunnel. I followed the tunnel for several hours until I saw rabbits in a large opening. They were having lunch. So they invited me in to have lunch with them. I didn't want to be rude so I joined them. They were eating green grass and some carrots. They offered me some kind of juice that I think was blackberry. I decided to leave when they began to make fun of my ears. They said they were small and looked silly. I left the rabbits and started home. It was not long and I saw a large lion. So I started running. I could hear something behind me and knew it must be the lion. I ran faster and soon I was so tired I could hardly run any farther. I looked back and did not see the lion. Instead I saw a small mouse chasing me. The lion must not have seen me but the mouse did. I guess he thought it was funny to chase me. I went home and stayed in my treehouse glad to be home."

The tribe sat stunned. They had never heard such a story. It was ridiculous and it did not make sense to them. Halmak stood up glaring at Talon. He did not say anything. He grasped his mate's hand pulling her up. They walked to the back of the cave. Talon said, raising his voice. "It's a jest."

Ela and Talon laid under the heavy buffalo skin that night.

"Talon, you should stop telling your jest stories. I do not understand why you say what you do." Ela said firmly.

"He rolled over pulling her close to him. He placed his lips against hers in his strange way then kissed her neck. "It was a true story."

"No it was not," she said as she felt the tingling of his lips on her neck. "You should tell stories that are true." She closed her eyes, feeling his body close to hers.

When the days became longer hunters would go out looking for food. It had been a long winter and all were anxious to get out of the cave. Many people did enjoy hearing Talon's stories. Although, there were those who did not want to hear them since they were not true. It was early spring when Ela told Talon she was with child. He and the cave were happy.

The days became longer and spring soon replaced the cold days. Hunters were soon out looking for large game to bring down. Women and children were out gathering fruit, vegetables, roots and herbs for the cave. It was a good time for the men and women of the tribe.

Young boys would go with Talon who taught them how to make fish traps as well as other traps for small animals. They learned to make a bow and arrows. Each of them practiced how to shoot. All of them learned where to find the rocks that sparked making fire. The young boys wanted to soon join the hunters.

When the weather became colder and the days shorter all of the tribe knew it would soon be time for the long winter months. Ela would give birth to a boy as it became cold. He looked like Talon. Food was smoked and placed in the cool part of the cave preparing for the long winter months.

Talon would often tell stories which intrigued the tribe. It was a cold night as Talon lay close to Ela who had the baby close to her. He suddenly felt a sharp pain in his head. He lay quiet then felt it again this time the pain did not go away. He pushed the covers back and stood up. The pain was more intense. He walked to the front of the cave. Pushing the large heavy hide back he stepped outside in the cold crisp air. The pain became sharper. He felt his body filled with pain. He bent over as his body began to shake then in an instant he was gone.

Chapter V

Beth looked up from her control panel when she saw the red light blinking and heard the alarm going off. She pressed the intercom button, "you better get in here!"

The room was suddenly filled with men and women running into the room. They were checking computer screens and looking at data. All of them were excited.

Joanne looked up "He's still alive. The chip has jumped him into another time zone."

An older man with gray hair walked in quickly going to Joanne. "What's happening Dr. Wright?"

"He's made a jump. He's the first one to jump to another time period."

"So he's alive?"

"Yes, if he were dead the chip would not have activated. It is charged from the electrical currents from his brain. Brian is alive."

"Where is he?" the older man asked anxiously.

Joanne looked at the data shaking her head. "I don't know. It's not where, it is when. I'm not sure how far back he went in time. I can tell you he is the first to go to another time period."

William Shakly sat back. He was concerned. He had not been for the project of sending people back into time. He was not sure how it was possible. The Scientist had figured out an equation from Albert Einstein making it possible to send a person back in time. Brian White was the third man they had sent back in time. He was the only one to move forward.

William leaned forward. "Okay now explain again how this chip works, and don't try and impress me with all your knowledge or vocabulary Doctor Wright."

Joanne smiled. "The chip in Brian's brain is equipped with a small transmitter that will activate and will be able to create a small black hole in a way that allows him to go from one period of time to another. He should be back here tomorrow. It will only be three days for us but it will be about ten years for him." Doctor Wright smiled "The chip is equipped with information from our computers. It will help Brian survive by translating language, and help him adapt to his current environment."

"So" William said as he concentrated, "He will live ten years in the past but return and it will only be a few days. What if he jumps into the future, say ten years from now?"

"I don't believe that will happen. The chip is programmed to come back to this specific time. It is possible to go into the future, but I believe it will happen as we planned. Brian will return to our time in this place"

William stood up. What about the other two James and Kevin?"

"I'm not sure sir. They may have died."

"I was not for this experiment and I am having a hard time with the budget committee explaining the amount of money spent on this project, which I cannot tell them about because it is classified. When Brian returns we will discuss this in depth. I believe many will find this unethical when it is revealed."

When William walked out of the room the men and women checked out the data trying to figure out where Brian was. He was somewhere in the past but where?

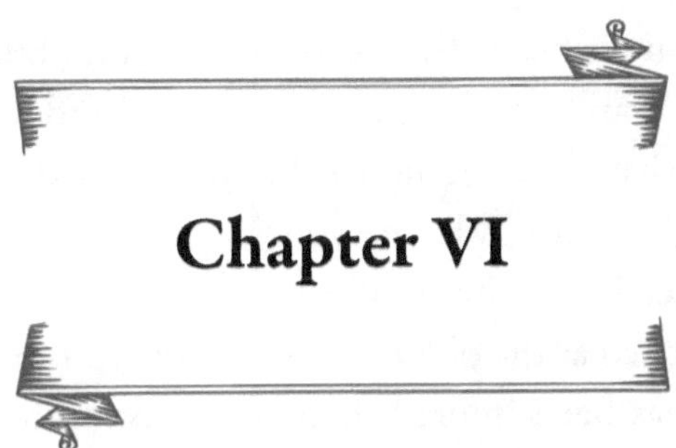

Chapter VI

Five Roman soldiers walking towards their camp on a dusty road slowed down seeing a naked man laying in the middle of the road. Gaius who was in charge of the patrol walked to the man bending over looking at him. "He looks like a Roman. Hebrews must have jumped him. I don't recognize him."

The other soldiers stared down at the man; none of them knew him. Gaius had two of the soldiers carry him the short distance to their camp.

Arriving at the camp the man was taken to the infirmary. Doctors checked him out without seeing any wounds. They were not sure why the man was unconscious. Gaius found the camp commander reporting the man being found. Decimus followed Gaius to the infirmary. He studied the man's face but did not recognize him.

"No doubt the Hebrews attacked him. They often will attack a Roman soldier who is alone. I hate them all and this wretched place." Decimus said as he turned to walk away.

The man woke up the following day. He was confused not knowing where he was. He remembered being in the cave next to Ela. Now he was in a strange place not understanding how he was in a strange new world. He did not speak as a man walked up looking into his eyes. "How are you feeling?" the man asked gruffly. He was an older man who was overweight and balding. The man did not answer. "What is your name, and where are you from?" He still did not answer, feeling pain throbbing in his head. The words were strange but he understood them. The older man looked at him then turned and walked away.

Decimus arrived later going to the man in bed. "I am Decimus, commander of the camp. Who are you?"

"I'm not sure," he said hesitantly.

Decimus looked at the older man standing next to him.

"His head has been injured. It is not uncommon for men to be confused after a severe head injury." The Doctor said quietly.

Decimus talked with the man who did not answer. He left irritated.

Two days later the Doctor had the man stand up and walk. He was released that afternoon. The Doctor could not find any injuries and he seemed to be doing better. He was taken to the commander.

"I will call you Perditus, that means lost. You seem to be lost and confused." Decimus said as he stood up from the couch. "Let's see what you can do, Perditus."

They walked to an open field where men were armed with bows. Decimus pointed to a bow, "pick up the bow and arrow and see if you can hit the target." He pointed to a target thirty meters away.

Perditus picked up the bow and an arrow. It felt comfortable in his hand. He drew the bow back holding the arrow in place. He released the string and the arrow flew, hitting the center of the target. He picked up another arrow, firing it at the target. The arrow landed close to the first. Decimus smiled. "You're an archer. There is no doubt."

They both walked to another area where men with wooden swords were practicing. "Gaius, see if this man can use a sword."

Gaius handed Perditus a wooden sword and shield. He swung his sword which Perditus blocked. After a short time Decimus shook his head.

"You may be an archer Perditus but you are no swordsman. Teach him to use the sword Gaius," he said walking away.

That night Perditus lay in his bed confused. He was trying to adjust to the new world he had found himself in. He was confused. He did not know how he could be where he was. He remembered Ela and the others. Hunting and working the hides. He missed Ela and wondered about his son. How was it possible to be in such a different place?

The days passed as Perditus, who had been called Talon in another time, adjusted to life in the garrison with the Roman soldiers. He went on patrol with Gaius who was in charge of the squad. They walked through the city of Nazarath making sure all was quiet. The Hebrews would always step out of the way when the soldiers approached. Perditus saw in the eyes of the people of the small village the hate and disgust they all felt for Roman soldiers. It made him feel uncomfortable. The squad would return in the evening to Sephoris.

Perditus had finished breakfast when Gaius walked up patting him on the shoulder. He had been in the Roman camp for seven months.

"Congratulations Perditus, you have been given a special assignment."

He stood up "what is the special assignment?"

Gaius smiled as he turned walking off, "follow me."

They walked into the town of Sephoris which was a large well kept city. It was a neat city where people of different nationalities were living and working. Gaius stopped in front of what looked like a cave with a large iron gate. A guard opened it and they both walked down steps into the cave. He stopped at a gate as another guard opened it. They walked into a small room that had been dug out of the rock. An older man in dirty robes sat on the floor. He looked up with tired eyes. He had long hair and a beard. Gaius picked up a chain and snapped it on Perditus' wrist.

"This is John, you will stay with him until the Governor in Jerusalem calls for him."

"I have to stay in this cell with this old man?" He asked surprised.

"Yes you do. The Governor wants him in chains until he is tried in Jerusalem. You will be his keeper. If he escapes then you will finish his sentence. The Governor will no doubt have him crucified." Gaius walked out of the cell shutting the door. "Enjoy yourself Perditus."

"How long do I have to stay here?"

"Until you take him to Jerusalem." Gaius said laughing as he walked away.

Perditus sat down looking at the old man. "So John, what did you do to be locked up?"

The old man looked up. "I was his disciple."

"Whose disciple?

"Jesus, I followed him and when the Romans killed him at the request of the temple leaders I continued to spread his message."

Perditus recognized the name of Jesus. His mind was racing. "Jesus, some say he was the messiah. He was crucified."

John looked at him curiously. "You have a strange accent for a Roman. Most Romans do not know Jesus since he died so long ago."

"John, you were with him when he died on the cross. He asked you to take care of Mary."

"Yes, he did. How did you know that? I don't believe you are old enough to have been there. I was a young man when he asked me to take care of his Mother."

"It's in the Bible."

"I don't understand what the Bible is?" John said, confused.

They sat quietly looking at each other.

"The Bible is a book that is inspired by God. The Old Testament is the stories of Abraham, Issac, Jacob and other men and women who the Lord used for his glory. The New Testament is the words of Jesus, and those who knew him. There is a book of John, one of Jesus's disciples."

John sat quiet as he tried to understand what this strange man was telling him. He had been writing the words of the Lord for many years. He wanted to remember the words Jesus spoke and his miracles. "Tell me more of this Bible." he said softly."

"Many of the books are written by Paul. He was Saul of Taurus. Other Disciples also wrote the New Testament which is the story of Jesus' birth, death and resurrection." Perditus said, looking at the old man.

John smiled, "I'm not sure of what you are saying. I knew Paul. He had been an enemy of the Church until Jesus spoke with him. He became a believer. He was a passionate man and died in Rome for his beliefs. I wonder if you are an angel sent from God?"

That evening John laid down after having a meager supper. Perditus laid next to the old man thinking how strange it was to be here. He thought of the Roman soldiers who he did not like. They were brutal to the people. They often bragged about beating the Hebrews and dragging them to jail if they could not pay their taxes. How they often beat and violated women. He was sick to his stomach thinking of the men who believed he was a Roman. He remembered Ela and her young son. He wondered about them and how he came to be in this place. He could not remember anything before. He sometimes in his dreams saw people in white coats and a strange room with machines. He dreamed of being in a uniform and had strange weapons. He could not remember his past.

As the days passed Perditus sat and talked with John who was a soft spoken man. He talked of Jesus and his miracles. Seeing him heal people and talking of love for all people. The guards were indifferent and when he asked how long he was to be in the cell. They would shrug their shoulders saying "as long as it takes for the Governor to call for you."

Chapter VII

Perditus had enough of the stinking cell. Lice and bugs crawling on him was driving him crazy. He had watched the guards being changed every twelve hours learning their routine. He decided he was leaving, he would not stay any longer in the dirty cell. He told John he was going to leave the cell and would be taking him with him. John had done nothing wrong except spread the message of Jesus. It was the authorities of the temple that were putting pressure on the Governor to silence him. He would not allow him to be killed.

That evening as it grew dark in the cell. The young man who had just come on duty opened the cell door sitting their dinner on the floor. Perditus stood up striking the man in the jaw. He went down hitting the hard floor on his face. Perditus with John chained to him stepped out of the cell shutting the door. The young man did not have the key to the chains so he was locked in the cell.

The men made their way up the stone steps to the top of the prison. John had shackles on his feet so he moved slowly. They walked to the iron gate. Perditus yelled "Open up!"

The outside guard placed a large key into the lock. As it opened Perditus pushed the gate open striking the guard. Perditus hit the man twice, knocking him out. He found the key to the chains and unlocked the chain on his wrist and John. He then removed the shackles from John.

"We must go see Mary. I need to make sure she is safe." John said softly. "I made a promise."

Perditus nodded his head. He removed the sword then pushed the guard inside the prison, shutting the door and locking it. Both men walked away from the prison.

The city was quiet with no lights on. It was late as people were asleep in their homes. They did hear laughing and talking as they passed by people in a large building drinking. The stars and moon were bright on the clear night. Leaving the city walking on the dusty road they headed east toward Nazarath. Neither spoke as they walked knowing if they were caught they would be executed.

The city of Nazarath was quiet and dark as they entered the small town. John led the way going to the east end of town. John stopped at a house that had a wall surrounding it. He knocked on the gate door. They both waited then heard the bolt sliding open. The door was opened and a woman holding a small oil lamp peered at the two strangers. Her eyes opened wide in recognition as she saw John. Her hand went to her mouth as tears streamed down her cheeks. She put her arm around his neck crying. Through her sobs she said "we thought you were dead John."

"Oh no Miriam I am alive by the grace of God. My friend helped me escape the prison."

Miriam looked at Perditus. She stepped back in fear seeing the Roman soldier standing next to John.

"He's okay Miriam, He helped me escape. He is not like the other soldiers. He has a kind heart." John said quickly.

MIriam was not sure what to think. She stepped back allowing the men to step inside. She shut the gate and grasped John's hand. She walked with him inside the small courtyard to the house.

Opening the door she said "Mother, John is here. It's a miracle!"

An elderly woman sitting in an old chair slowly stood up and walked to John. She put her arms around him hugging his neck. She kissed his cheek and said

"our prayers have been answered. You are safe John."

John smiled as he looked at Mary. "I believe God has spared me for a time, Mary, how are you feeling?"

She took his hand leading him to a chair, where he sat down. "I am good now that I know you are safe my friend. How did you get out of prison?"

John looked not seeing Perditus. "I was helped by a Roman soldier who was chained to me. I believe he may be an angel from the Lord. He has a knowledge that I can not explain."

Perditus had seen the fear in Miriam's eyes and knew she was afraid of him. When John went into the house he stayed outside. He sat down on a bench not wanting to impose on people who were afraid of him. He was not sure what he would do and was thinking of his next move when the door opened and a small woman walked outside holding an oil lamp.

She had a scarf covering her head. Her gray hair hung loosely on her back. Her dark eyes had wrinkles around them. She did not smile as she looked at Perditus. She spoke just above a whisper. "You are welcomed in my home. John has told me how you saved him. Please come inside."

The woman turned and walked inside the house. Perditus followed the small older women inside. He sat on an old couch and watched as a young girl walked up to him carrying a bowl of water. She sat it down and began to wash his feet.

"You don't have to do that. I can do it."

The young girl watched surprised as the man took the rag and began washing his feet. He also washed his face and neck. When he was through, the young girl picked up the bowl and walked away.

Mary had watched the man as she sat quietly in her chair.

"You do not know our customs. It was the young girl's duty to wash a guest's feet."

"I didn't mean to offend you. It didn't seem right for the young girl to wash my feet when I am capable of doing it myself."

The older woman sat quietly studying him. "John said your name is Perditus, that means lost in Latin. How did you come by this name? Where are you from?"

"I don't have any memory of where I am from, or what my name is. The camp commander gave me the name Perditus." He looked at the older woman then spoke in a low voice. "You are the virgin Mary. Your son was Jesus, some believe is the Messiah."

Mary smiled slightly. "You know of my son. Do you accept him as the messiah?"

"I know of your son." He spoke quietly

"I was a virgin when I married Joseph, and gave birth without knowing a man. I have sons and daughters so to call me a virgin would not be correct."

"I apologize if I offended you." He looked down.

Mary watched him then said "You are a Roman soldier, but you show such respect."

"I am dressed as a Roman soldier. I do not remember who I am. The Romans believed I was Roman since I look like thém. I do not think I am Roman. I'm not sure who I am."

Mary stood up "you will sleep on the roof it is cooler. I will see you in the morning."

She showed Perditus where the ladder was then left. He climbed the ladder and lay down next to John. He stared at the stars until he fell asleep.

Chapter VIII

The following morning when Preditus woke the sun was shining. He was the only one on the roof. He sat up tossing the light blanket off, then stood up making his way to the ladder leading inside the small house. Mary was the only person in the house. She watched as he washed his hands, face and neck. He washed his hair and dried off with a small towel. She stood up pointing to the couch. Peditus sat down as she brought him food. She sat down staring intently at him.

He looked out the window seeing a large group of people.

"They have come to see John. He has told them of how you helped him escape. Some believe you are an angel. Others do not trust you since you are Roman."

"What do you believe?" he asked as he drank the warm milk.

"You are strange." she said not smiling.

They sat quietly as he ate. When he finished Mary took the plate and cup sitting it on the table. Peditus looked at her. She was older but still attractive. He sat back saying "you could not find your son so you and your husband looked for him. He was in the temple talking with the priest."

"How do you know this? Joseph and I were worried. We searched for him and when we found him he was in the courtyard teaching the priest's. He was so young."

"I read it in the Bible." He sat up "It is a book where I am from that many believers read."

"Where is it you are from?"

"I don't know. I can not remember." He sat looking at Mary feeling awe talking to her.

"Jesus was special." She said, speaking softly. "He was a good boy who learned his father's trade. He was a good carpenter, perhaps not as talented as Joseph. Jesus was a good child. He often was alone. I would find him near the creek sitting and looking into the water. He helped with the younger children. Joseph took him to work with him where he learned his trade. I loved him. He left and began his ministry. I had to let him go, although I wanted him to stay."

"His first miracle was at your request. He turned water into wine."

"It was at my cousin's wedding. They had run out of wine which was a shame for them. It truly was a miracle. He was blessed and healed many people."

"He is loved and many follow him." Perditus said, looking at Mary who sat watching him.

"You will have to leave, it is not safe here. The soldiers will be looking for you and John. You need to take care of him."

"I will do my best."

Miriam came into the house smiling. "John is feeling better. He is telling the people of Jesus."

"That's what he does." Mary said, looking at her. "This is my daughter. Miriam. Her husband Ezikal and their children stay with me."

Perditus smiled, "It is a pleasure to meet you Miram."

When it was dark John and Perditus prepared to leave. Mary hugged John, telling him good by knowing it was the last time she would see her friend. She looked at Perdius and hugged him, kissing him on the cheek.

"You will need to be careful. There will be soldiers looking for you both."

They walked out of the house and down the dusty road. It was late and both knew it was going to be a dangerous trip. They would travel to Ephesus where there were many believers.

The men walked slowly as John was older. He told of being a fisherman with his brother James. How they left their boats to follow Jesus. He had no regrets. He talked of the disciples and how he loved them. They sat to rest as John seemed to be lost in his thoughts.

"They're all gone. The eleven and I who chose to follow Jesus. Judas hanged himself when he betrayed Jesus. He believed Jesus would lead a rebellion against the Romans. When it became apparent that was not the Lord's mission. He received thirty pieces of silver for telling the authorities where Jesus was." John bowed his head as the tears fell. "We all ran when they came for him."

Pedritus sat quietly as John sat weeping. He felt the old man's pain. It had been so many years ago, but he still grieved.

John looked up. "I am the last. All of the others are gone. Killed by the Romans. I'm not sure why I have been spared but I have been."

When they met men along the way Pedritus said he was taking a Hebrew prisoner to the Governor. Since he was in a Roman uniform no one questioned him. They stayed at houses along the way. John knew many people and they were glad to allow him to stay. Sometimes they would stay in a small inn. Pedritus would tell the innkeeper to send his bill to the Roman Governor. No one questioned him.

They rested at a home in the country. Both men were tired and needed rest. In the evening when it was cool Perditus asked, "John there were many who followed Jesus, it must have taken a lot of money to feed all the people?"

"Yes, there were many that followed Jesus and the twelve of us. Some of the followers were wealthy and provided funding. Mary Magdalene was one who helped support the message. She was troubled when she came to the Lord. He removed evil spirits that had bothered her for years. She was special and was a good apostle." He sat quietly for some time then said. "We were jealous of her. The Lord taught her and she was close to him. Mary was a wonderful teacher. She was kind and caring. She was able to heal the sick and lame the same as Jesus. I regret being so petty and being jealous of her. Jesus appeared to her first after he lay in the tomb for three days. Then to the rest of us later. She was special as we all were to Jesus. We realized that after he went to be with his Father. I have lost contact with Mary, I don't know where she is. I pray for her."

They traveled for weeks on the dusty road heading for Caesarea. They planned to arrive in the port city and take a boat to Ephesus. It was late and they were not able to find a house to stay in. John said they would be in Caesarea by evening the following day.

Perditus built a fire and had a meal of goat meat they had been given in the last house they stayed in. Perditus looked up hearing horses on the road. It was dark and he could not tell who they were.

Twelve Roman soldiers walked into the camp. They looked at the two men.

"I am Gaius from Sephoris." Perditus said standing up.

"Caeso" a man who was in charge said "and these surely looking thugs are my men."

"Good to meet you, Caeso. This ruffian is John. I am escorting him to Rome."

The men all sat down by the fire looking at John and Perditus.

"Why are you taking him to Rome?" A young man asked, looking at John with contempt."

"He's a Hebrew. Isn't that enough?"

The men laughed. The young man looked at Perditus suspiciously. "So Who is the Commander in Sephoris?"

"Decimus. He's a cantankerous man who would rather be in Rome. He does not seem to like the Hebrews. I don't believe they like him much either."

The men all laughed as they opened a flask of wine passing it around.

The young man did not laugh. "Why isn't this prisoner in chains? All prisoners are to be chained when escorted."

"He's an old man. If he runs off I will catch him."

The men laughed, one of them saying "you need to calm down centurion. You're not in Rome."

The men drank until the wine was gone. They were soon asleep by the fire.

When it was getting light Perditus rose silently and woke John. They left before the Roman soldiers woke up.

They arrived in Caesarea by early evening. A merchant ship was leaving for Ephesus the following morning. The captain was a Hebrew and knew of John. He was happy to take the old man on his ship.

It would be a long journey but the weather was pleasant. John talked with the sailors of Jesus and his message. Sitting on board the ship as the evening became cool John said "I am glad the weather is calm. The sea can be dangerous with storms that appear suddenly."

Perditus smiled saying "You could command the sea to be quiet as Jesus did."

John's eyes narrowed "I was there and was scared more than I had ever been in my life. The boat was about to sink and Peter woke Jesus. He looked at us in disgust and told the storm to cease. It did immediately. We knew he was truly the Son of God." John asked "How did you know this story? You must have heard it but most do not believe it."

"I read it in the bible. It also tells of Jesus walking on the water."John sat back looking at Perditus as he smiled and continued. "In the bible is a story of Jesus walking on the water. It was during a storm. When the Disciples saw Jesus walking on the water they thought he was a spirit. Peter called out to him, and Jesus told him to come to him. Peter stepped out and walked on the water for a while until he took his eyes off Jesus." Pedritus smiled, watching John.

John said nothing. The sailors asked John if it was true. He told them it was then used the story as a lesson for having faith, believing in the impossible.

They would arrive in Ephesus where John had friends that took him in. They felt safe being away from the Romans. John would have visitors every day and would spend his days preaching to those who wanted to hear the old apostle. He was the last who had walked with Jesus and had heard his message. He told of the miracles and his love. The crowd would sit quietly listening to the soft but strong voice of John.

One evening as Perditus lay in his bed he felt a shooting pain in his head. He staggered outside, going to his knees. His body began to shake then in an instant he was gone.

Chapter IX

He woke up looking around seeing men laying on the ground. Confused and his head hurting he did not know where he was. He tried to sit up but his head was throbbing. He lay back down on the ground. The sound of men in pain was sickening. Many were crying while others were praying. He sat up as his head hurt. He was sickened by the sight of so many dead men. Many were wounded. He realized he was naked.

A man approached him. He looked him over asking in a strong English accent "where are you hurt?"

He didn't say anything but looked blankly at the man. The man pushed him down and went to the next man looking him over. He was dead. The smell of death hung heavy in the air. He closed his eyes and fell asleep.

He woke up as a man was shaking him roughly. "Why are you naked," a young man asked? The man shook his head sitting up. "I don't know?"

"What is your name? What company are you with?"

He was confused and said "John," He was going to ask where John was but the young man who was impatient asked "Who do you fight with John?"

"I don't know?" He said softly.

The young man handed him some clothes that were dirty and too big for him.

"Get dressed, you are capable of fighting."

John stood up putting on pants and a shirt. He was led with other men by the young man. They stopped in front of a large tent. A big man walked out. He looked at the men and asked "Where do you fight?

One of the men said he was an archer. John said "I'm an archer."

The other men mumbled where they had been before being hurt.

John and five other men were taken through the camp to an area where men sat silently around fires. He sat down and accepted a bowl of stew. He did not have a spoon so he used his fingers and drank the watery stew. The men sat talking in low tones of the battle they would fight in the morning. One man who had a beard and was filthy said "We will take Acre tomorrow." The others nodded grimly.

The following day as the sun was rising John with the other men were given a bow and a quiver of arrows. They walked to an area where John could see a large wall around a city. He was confused wondering where he was. He heard a man bark an order. He watched as men removed an arrow and placed it on the string pulling it back and pointing it in the air. He did the same. Another order and the arrows were released. He watched as hundreds of arrows flew into the city. The men continued to fire arrows, so he did the same. An order was barked and the archers stopped.

John watched as men with swords and long pikes raced for the city. They were soon inside and the battle he heard was horrible. The archers with their bows on their backs with their arrows, pulled their swords. Soon they were racing for the city. John ran with the men not sure what he was supposed to do. Once inside the city he saw men locked in a terrible conflict.

John remained in the back with the archers. Soon horses with men in armor raced inside the city. The battle soon ended. The men of the city surrendered. John and the other archers were taken to the far end of the city. There he saw men, women, and children sitting against the wall. He was told to watch the prisoners and not allow them to escape. He was still confused and wondered what was going on.

The prisoners were dark skinned people. LIstening to the men talk he realized they were Muslim. The English were fighting in the Holy Land with the goal of taking the city of Jerusalem. He realized he was fighting in the crusades under King Richard I of England.

John fell into a routine as the weeks went by. He would stand guard watching the prisoners from the fallen city. He watched as the children played. Women would not look at him. The men had nothing but contempt for him. He would be relieved in the evening going with the rest of the men to where they were camped. The rumor was King Richard was negotiating for a prisoner exchange. The men in the camp did not speak much so John, who was quiet, sat and tried to understand what was happening to him. He remembered Ela and the cave. He missed her and his son. He thought of John who he came to respect. Now he was in a war that did not make sense.

One afternoon men arrived saying all prisoners were to be brought to the front wall. The three thousand men, women, and children were gathered together and marched to the front wall. John could see the opposing army outside. He was shocked as men were taken to the top of the wall and killed. Swords were driven through them and their bodies thrown to the ground. More men were dragged up the steps and they were also killed. He was sick when he saw women who were screaming and crying dragged up the steps standing on the wall. Their heads were cut off and thrown down. Children were also dragged up the steps to the wall. He was in shock seeing so many men, women, and children murdered.

The Muslim army attacked. He and other archers fired arrows into the air. They rained down bringing death. The soldiers for King Richard attacked, defeating the Muslim army. It was a sickening sight seeing so many dead men lying in the battlefield including the men, women, and children lying near the wall.

Only a few of the women and children were spared. Twenty six hundred men, women, and children were killed. The army moved out when the Muslim army was reinforced.

The army moved south. They set up camp near the city of Arsuf. Soon the Crusaders were surrounded by the Muslim army. King Richard set up his defenses and waited. They were outnumbered and all feared the army would be overrun.

The Crusaders put up a fight and when it was over the Crusaders had won a major victory. The fighting was terrible and the casualties on both sides were tremendous. John had remembered his lessons as a Roman Soldier and how to wield his sword. He fought hard and watched as many of the enemy fell. He also saw many of those he had known also die. The battle was terrible. The cost of the battle was high in life. The Muslim army withdrew. Too many had died. John was sick as he sat quietly drinking water that was stale. He did not feel like eating as he lay down next to the fire slowly going out. It was hot in the daytime and the evenings were not much cooler. The smell of death hung in the air.

The Army moved toward Jerusalem. Saladin with his Muslim Army blocked the road. The Crusaders were able to take several small fortresses. They were only a few miles from Jerusalem.

On the Sabbath day the army rested. Since it was so large several Priests had to conduct separate services. The elite knights with King Richard were in a group and the rest of the army was split into smaller groups so services could be conducted.

John sat with the infantry and archers as a Priest began the services. He looked around seeing men sitting silently as the Priest spoke in Latin. He realized most of the men did not speak Latin. The Priest spoke of the great day the city of God would be returned to the Christians. John was becoming more irritated as he heard the Priest talk of how the Lord was with them in this holy pursuit.

John was near the front and as the Priest paused he yelled "What about Jesus?"

The Priest was surprised at being interrupted. John stood up. "Why are you speaking in Latin when most here do not understand Latin?"

"The Holy Word of God is to be spoken in Latin!" The Priest said angrily.

"Latin is the language of the Romans who killed Jesus. You speak of hate and killing from the Old Testament Priest. Jesus came to fulfill the old covenant not destroy it. What about loving your enemy? The Muslims did not kill Jesus."

The Priest was shocked. "That is blasphemy! How dare you interrupt this message with Heresy!"

"You condone the killing of women and children who are innocent. Do you believe Jesus would approve? Heresy is on you Pharisee!"

John was arrested and placed in chains.

John sat silently with heavy chains on him. He remembered the chains he wore when he was with John. He silently prayed and waited for death. He was surprised as five men walked up to him. They were well dressed. The taller man was wearing a small crown on his head.

The taller man looked at him for a while then said. "I understand you are a good fighter. Your commanders say you fight with passion. Why is it you question the word of our Lord?"

John knew it was King Richard who was speaking to him. He also was aware the men with him were his knights. Behind them were several Priests.

"Sire, I don't question the holy word. I was questioning the Priest who was speaking in Latin and most men don't understand that language. I simply wanted to know what is wrong with the King's language. All of the men in the army know it well."

King Richard smiled slightly. "Latin is the language used to bring the word."

"Jesus spoke Aramaic. Why not use that language?"

King Richard turned to the Priest behind him. "Did Jesus speak Aramac?"

The Priest was visibly angry. "Yes Sire, the Holy Father has decreed Latin is to be used in bringing the holy word."

"The Romans spoke Latin. They crucified Jesus." John said, looking at the Priest.

"Blasphemy! You speak Blasphemy! The priests all yelled.

"How do you know the word of the Lord so well? Are you a Priest?" King Richard asked.

"The words and languages are in my head. I understand languages and the word. Paul spoke of gifts from the Holy Spirit. Speaking in tongues is a gift. That is when a person understands different languages." He looked at the Priest. "You do understand when the Apostle Paul said language that is not understood without an interpreter is nothing but a gong clanging, an empty barrel."

The priest's face was red as he stared at John. "I want this man executed for blasphemy!"

"I'm a prophet." John said, staring at King Richard. "Jesus said as he looked down from the same hill he would be crucified on, "Jerusalem I weep for you since you killed the Prophets of the Lord."

The Priest was shocked. "You will die for this Heresy."

King Richard and his men who were all educated understood the exchange.

"I decide who dies, Priest. You don't give that order."

"He is a heretic, Sire." The priest protested, raising his voice.

"He is also a fierce fighter according to his commander." He looked at John, "Tell me Prophet will we take Jerusalem?"

"No, the Lord will not allow that since you're with a false Priest. You should be more concerned with your kingdom in England. You have been gone for a long time Sire."

Richard stared hard at John. He was concerned with reports he was hearing from his kingdom. He looked at the men beside him.

"Release the prophet, we will need fighting men." he looked at John. "you will not interrupt any services in the future."

"Yes Sire." John said, looking down.

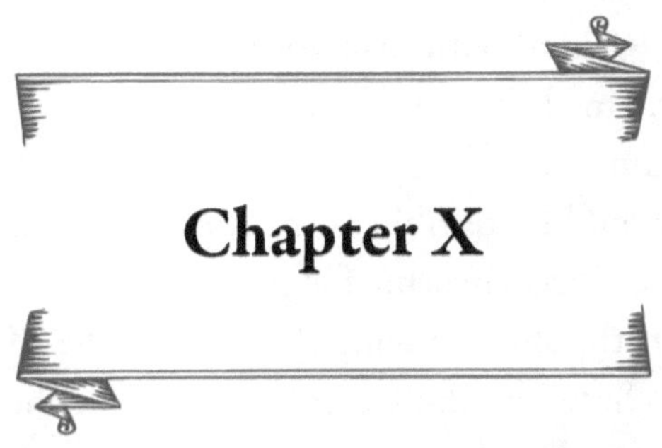

Chapter X

King Richard began negotiations with Saladen. The negotiations would drag on throughout the winter. It was a tedious time for the army to set and wait. The Priest's were furious that the King was negotiating with the Muslims. They were so close to Jerusalem they could take it. King Richard however, did not seem interested. He preferred to negotiate with Saladen.

The talks resulted in King Richard not taking Jerusalem. Saladen agreed to allow Christians to go to the holy city and not be bothered. This was not what the Priest's wanted. They wanted Jerusalem to be in the hands of Christians. When John reminded the Priest Jesus was not a Christian, he was Jewish they demanded he be executed. King Richard ignored them.

King Richard prepared to leave for home. He was anxious to return to his kingdom. He had been gone for years and was worried there could be problems back home. His plans would change when the report of Jaffa being taken by Muslim forces. The city had been overrun and the Crusaders were trying to hold the city. A small number of men were holding out as the rest were tortured and murdered. It was retaliation for the massacre at Acre. King Richard had a decision to make. Should he sail home, or take Jaffe rescuing the men in the city.

KIng Richard with two thousand men sailed for Jaffe. When the Turks saw the ships heading for Jaffe they rallied and all of them raced for the shore. The Muslim Army outnumbered the Christians ten to one. The Turks filled the shores with so many men hoping to prevent a landing. King Richard with his sword, shield, and crossbow jumped from the boat and made his way to shore. The rest of the army including John followed him.

The battle would be terrible as the two armies clashed. Although outnumbered the Christian army fought hard and was able to push the Muslim army off the shore. Seeing their defeat the Muslim turned to run. They were chased by the Christians who cut them down. It was a terrible defeat for the Muslim army who were confident they could defeat a smaller force. The city of Jaffe was returned to the Crusaders.

John sat on the beach exhausted. He had fought alongside other Crusaders who had defeated the Turks. He was sickened upon hearing how the Turks had tortured wounded Crusaders. It was sad to think how men could treat other men. He lay down thinking of the Massacre at Acre. It was a terrible thing to watch. He was sure the Lord was not pleased.

THE FOLLOWING DAY FOUR men came to John and escorted him to the city. He walked into one of the few buildings standing. The room where he was taken was well furnished. He saw several men standing and talking. He knew King Richard was the center of attention. Several of the Priests were also there. He waited patiently at the back of the room.

King Richard turned and motioned for him to approach. The four men on each side walked with him to the King.

"You fought well in the recent battle. You are to be commended. The city of Jaffe is now in the hands of Christians."

John did not say anything as he felt scared knowing he was no doubt in trouble.

"I regret to inform you Prophet you will be executed in the morning. You have been talking with the men and many of them are questioning the Priest and their services. I cannot allow problems in my army."

"I fought for you, and now you want to execute me? That seems rude on your part, Sire." John said not smiling.

King Richard looked at him curiously. "Your talk of heresy is undermining morale. I will not allow you to speak out against Religion."

John looked at the Priest "will you have me crucified?"

"That is blasphemy! Your head will be removed for this Heresy." A Priest said as he stepped forward.

John spoke in Latin, "You are a wolf in sheep's clothing. You do not represent Jesus. When you stand before him he will say you have received your reward on Earth not in the kingdom of God, Pharisee."

The Priest was shaking, he was so angry. "You are excommunicated! You will burn in hell!"

"Thank you, when I meet Jesus and am judged he will see I was not a part of your twisted religion, that you have perverted. Jesus came to save sinners. You have made yourself fat on the poor. Your lust for power is sick. You want Jerusalem so you can rule as Caiaphas did many years ago" John said calmly.

The Priest's were shocked. King Richard held up his hand, "enough." He looked at John, "I do regret having to order your death. I believe you are intelligent. I cannot allow you to undermine Religion. You will die in the morning. May God be with you Prophet."

The following day when the door was opened John was not in the cell. He seemed to have vanished.

Chapter XI

He had been found on the beach. Two French soldiers picked him up and carried him to their camp. The Doctor examined him, not able to find any injuries. When he woke up he was confused. He was once again in a strange place. He heard two of the orderlies talking. They were speaking French. He could understand them. He was not sure how he understood French but he could. His head hurt and the pain was a constant low throbbing. He heard one of the men talk of his father Aubert who was a baker. He talked of missing good meals while serving in the army.

When the small doctor walked up seeing him awake he asked, "how do you feel?"

The man shook his head. "My head hurts."

"What is your name, and where are you from?"

"Robin Hode, I was a soldier in the recent crusades with King Richard."

The young Doctor smiled, "The Crusades with King Richard. Well I do remember studying the crusades in school. I believe that was a long time ago, perhaps 1200. He continued smiling. "Well, Robin, you were found near the beach. You did not have any clothes on. Why were you naked?"

"I don't know, I don't remember anything."

"I understand it is not uncommon for memory loss if there is a head injury, or perhaps you drank too much. I don't believe you are a crazy man, but I will have the orderlies watch you closely. " The Doctor said, continuing to smile.

"I don't believe I had too much to drink since I do not drink? I may be crazy. "

The small man said "we will release you in a few days. You will return to your unit."

Robin nodded without speaking. He was again confused. He remembered being in a cell in Jaffe. King Richard was going to have him executed. He lay back looking up at the ceiling. He was not sure what to think. Why was he moving from one time period to another? He thought of Ela and missed her. He wondered about his son. Were they okay? Would he return to them? He thought of John and wondered about the older man he had come to respect. His mind raced as he lay in his cot wondering if he was dreaming. Why was this happening to him?

Robin was released from the hospital the following day. He was taken to a unit where he learned how to load a long muzzle rifle. He had plenty of time to practice since the French army was waiting to move. There were many drills and marching throughout the day. Robin was often in trouble with his superiors since he did not know the drills. He soon caught on and was marching as well as most of the new recruits.

Early one morning the French army moved out. They were heading for the coast, and Terre-de-Haut island. It was in the coastal city where Fort Napoleon was located. Robin learned with the other recruits that they would be sailing for Egypt. Napoleon had been planning on invading Egypt in order to establish a French presence in the middle east. Napoleon hoped it would also hurt the English economy by limiting their Navel power.

The Army boarded ships after several months of waiting on the small island. They were on their way to Egypt. All of the army hoped to avoid the powerful English navy. Each Frenchman knew if the English

Navy found them the campaign would be over. The French knew they would not be able to withstand a fight with the English on the sea.

On board the ships were many scientists, artists, and other scholars. It was Napoleon's desire to not only conquer Egypt, but to document the history of the Middle East. The expedition would elevate Napoleon since he had been elected into the French Academy of Sciences. He would be recognised as an academic as well as a conqueror.

The ships did have pleasant weather. It would take two months to complete the journey. One evening as the men sat and talked Robin was asked about his family and where he was from. He sat for a while not sure what to say.

He finally said "I was raised on the coast. I remember one day I was fishing with a pole and a line. I snagged a huge fish. It put up a mighty fight almost dragging me into the sea. I fought the fish for hours finally being able to drag it to shore. The fish was the biggest I had ever seen. When I cut the belly open a little man jumped out. He scared me to death. He said he had been swallowed by the fish years ago. I grabbed my pole and chased the little man around the beach hitting him on the head and shoulders. I was able to chase him back into the sea. I cleaned the fish and when I took it to the village we ate the fish for six months."

The men laughed at the wild story. No one believed the fish tale. Robin insisted it was true. Jaque Delemon, a scientist said "Now Robin that is not true. You are speaking of Jonah and the whale. That is a bible story from over two thousand years ago."

"Well maybe it was Jonah's grandson. He could have been swallowed. Like dear old Grand Pappy." Robin said grinning.

The men continued to laugh as they talked of the story.

When the ships arrived in Malta they found little resistance. The victory gave the French army a moral victory and emboldened them for the campaign in Egypt. Robin did not see any action as it was mostly a skirmish. He did fight in the battle of Shubra Khit against the Malmkus calvary. They were slaves as well as freed slaves who fought for the ruling cast. The French army was able to secure a victory and more importantly were able to gain skills in fighting. This would prepare them for the battle of the pyramids.

The French army defeated the city of Alexendra then prepared to march across the desert. It was a difficult journey across the hot arid sand. The men suffered the scorching heat in the daytime and shivered in the cold nights. Napoleon pushed his army across the burning sands of the desert. The men suffered terribly as none of them knew what a dessert was. When the army entered Caraio they knew what heat and thirst was. They found outside of Caraio the Ottoman Army waiting for them.

The Ottoman Army was well equipped and had close to the same number of men the French Army had in its ranks.

Twenty five thousand French soldiers faced the Ottoman army of twenty nine thousand Mamluk Cavalry. The battle would be fierce.

Robin stood close to his companions in the newly enacted divisional square. Napoleon had invented the move to repel the Mamluk Cavalry. Napoleon believed the new tactic would be effective in preventing the cavalry from moving through the lines and attacking his rear. The men stood close together as the Cavalry attacked. He felt the fear washing over him as men on horseback charged. The men in the large rectangular formation were able to repel the charge. The cavalry would regroup each time and return. The French men stood strong as each of the cavalry charges were beaten back.

Robin felt sick as he looked over the battlefield. The dead men and horses were strewn across the sand. It was a decisive victory for the French who lost three hundred men. The Mamluk Cavalry lost over three thousand men. The Ottoman army was demolished. They retreated leaving the battlefield fleeing to upper Egypt.

The army rested in the shadow of the pyramids. The scientist's and artists along with the other academics went to work studying the huge pyramids. It was later the army heard that Heriatio Nelson leading the

English Navy defeated the French at the battle of the Nile. All but two ships were destroyed. The French army had defeated the Ottoman empire. However, there was still resistance as they fought back in small bands of men.

The army would rest for six months as the scientists made numerous discoveries. This would include the discovery of the Roseta stone. The stone with Greek writing as well as the strange hieroglyphs of the ancient Egyptians would allow archaeologists to decipher the writing of the Egyptians.

Robin was sick of the French army and the tyrannical Napoleon. He wanted to go back to Ela, and her son. He thought of her and wondered about her and their son. He was confused and depressed. He sat alone not talking to the other soldiers. He slowly rose when the order came to move out. The army was heading for Demascus.

The army was successful as it moved along the coast taking the cities of Arisha Gaza then Jaffa. Robin looked at the city of Jaffa. He remembered well the battle under

KIng Richard and the tremendous loss of life. He sat quietly staring into the fire when he heard his commander say.

"When we take Jaffa all men are to be killed with the bayonet. We do not want to waste bullets on the scum. Many of the men were paroled after being captured. They chose to fight again. Which is breaking their promise not to fight against our glorious leader. They will die a traitor's death."

Robin looked up at the commander as he sat. "Does that include women and children? Does our glorious leader want babies brought to him on the end of a bayonet?"

The commander glared at Robin then turned on his heel and walked away.

The following day Jaffa was taken. Many of the men were bayoneted or drowned. The French army attacked with enthusiasm.

For three days the men ran amok as they looted and harassed the men, women, and children of Jaffa.

Robin walked out of the city with his musket on his shoulder. He stopped and stared at Napoleon as he sat on his horse. He could see the gleam in his eye. He was enjoying the slaughter. Robin walked back to the camp and laid down. He was exhausted and wanted to die. He was tired of the bloodshed.

Later Robin watched as the army approached Acher. He remembered the massacre of the civilians in Acer, then how the muslims surrounded King Richard's army. The French army attacked the fort, however, it could not be taken. Napoleon turned his army and marched toward Cairo. The army was exhausted and many had died. Soon a plague ravished the army. Robin was horrified as the army Doctors under orders of Napoleon ordered the sick to be given large doses of opium. Hundreds died on the road back to Cario.

Napoleon would learn of problems in France. He would leave the army and sail back to France, taking the scientists with him. Robin hoped the English Navy would find him on the high seas and send him to the bottom of the ocean. Napoleon would return to France and be welcomed as a hero.

Robin felt the familiar pain in his head and soon he would be gone. The French soldiers thought he had deserted as so many had during the harsh campaign.

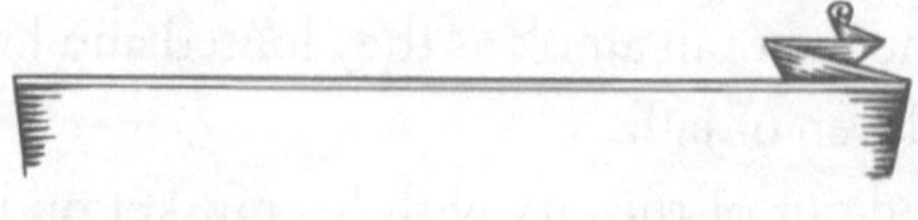

Chapter XII

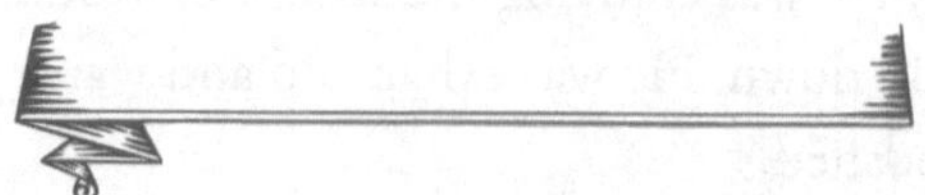

He opened his eyes in the dimly lit room. He was in bed and was confused. Not sure where he was. The room was small and the bed soft. He realized he was no longer in Egypt in the French army. Where was he? What was happening? Why was he moving through time? Nothing made sense.

A woman walked into the room. She was not tall, about five foot four, long brown hair and a pretty face. She smiled seeing the man brought to her two days ago was awake. "I'm glad to see you awake. How are you feeling?"

He didn't speak as he looked at the woman who was pretty.

"I'll send for the Doctor." She placed her soft hand on his forehead as her dark brown eyes stared intently into his. She poured him a cup of water and held his head as he drank the cool water. He watched her leave the room.

Later a young man walked into the room. "I'm Doctor Tally. Do you hurt anywhere?"

"My head hurts." He said softly.

"I'm not seeing any injuries. Can you tell me what happened?"

"I don't remember."

"I imagine you have a head injury. You were found on the prairie naked. You may have been attacked by Indiands, or bandits. You will heal. What is your name?"

He lay quite not sure which name he should use. He could not remember his name. "John." He whispered.

"Okay John I'll leave you now, but if you are feeling ill or have any problems let Ivy know." The Doctor walked out of the room.

"I will bring you some soup. I imagine you're hungry." The pretty woman said. She returned sitting in a chair next to the bed and with a large spoon began feeding him. It was good and he was hungry. The woman was quiet and did not speak much.

"Where am I," He asked,

"You're in my boarding house. I'm Ivy Green. Men found you outside of town and the Doctor had you brought here since Guthrie does not have a hospital."

He wanted to ask more but chose to remain quiet. "I can't pay you," He said embarrassed.

Ivy smiled "When you get on your feet there are jobs available. You can pay me then."

Two days later John was feeling better. He walked out of his small room into a large open space where a long table with chairs were set up. He was wearing a long night shirt. Men were sitting eating breakfast.

Ivy smiled standing up. "I'm glad to see you, John. Come have breakfast."

John walked with Ivy to the table sitting down. She brought him a plate and a fork. then handed him a platter of scrambled eggs and placed some on his plate. She put a biscuit on the plate and poured gravy over it. She smiled as she poured him coffee in a tin cup. The men asked him questions which he answered the best he could.

The men staying at the boarding house had a variety of different occupations. Some were salesmen, others worked for the railroad, or construction. The breakfast was good and he ate heartily. When it was over the men all stood up leaving. He helped Ivy clean the table and wash the dishes.

Ivy went to her room and returned with some men's clothes. She explained her husband had left and was not sure if he would return. She gave him the clothes saying "I think his clothes will fit you until you can get some of your own."

"Thank you." He said looking down.

John found Ivy sitting on the front porch after he had changed. She smiled,

"I'm glad the clothes fit you. They may be a little big."

John sat down in a chair next to Ivy. "I appreciate everything you have done."

She smiled at him "you were in need it is only right to help someone in need.

Ivy told him of how she and her husband Dave had come to Indian Territory for the run. Dave had been able to get a lot which he built the house knowing men would need somewhere to stay. He was a man who had big dreams and after a while he left. She was not sure if he was alive.

John knew that Indians across the country had been moved to Indian Territory by the US Government. They had been forced off their land which was resettled by white settlers. He was not sure how he knew there was land called unassigned land that was opened to settlers. He sat quietly for a while then said. "I'll go look for a job so I can pay my way."

Ivy smiled "There is a lot of building going on in Guthrie. I'm sure you will find a job."

John walked on wooden sidewalks hearing his boots that were too big echoing off the wood. The town was mostly wood structures. There were some tents erected. There were several businesses. Men and women were crowding the streets riding horses, mules, or in wagons.

He saw in an open space men laying bricks. He walked up to a man carrying bricks on a pole with wood in a V shape with bricks on them.

He asked "are there jobs available?" The man slowed then pointed to a man with a barrel chest laying bricks.

John walked up to the man bent over laying bricks.

"I'm looking for a job and was wondering if you were hiring?"

The man stood up looking at John.

"Ever mixed cement?"

"No."

The man frowned then sat his trowel down.

"Come with me."

John followed the man to a large wooden box. He picked up a shovel

"This is cement. Put in five shovels."

John watched the man put in five shovels of the gray powder. He walked to a pile of sand. "Put in ten shovels of sand." When the man was finished he sat the shovel down and picked up a hoe.

"Chop it up."

John watched the man mix the sand and cement with the hoe. He then put in five more shovels of cement and ten more shovels of sand. Taking the hoe he mixed it up thoroughly.

Picking up water he said "Add water, be careful do not add too much water."

John watched the man add water then mixed it with a hoe. He added more water and continued to mix it together.

The man laid the hoe down then picked up a shovel and began putting the cement in a wheelbarrow.

"Mix the cement the same way every time. If too much water is added then I can't lay bricks because it runs over. If it's too stiff it's hard to work with. Do you understand?"

"Yes.

When the wheelbarrow was full he pushed it to the building. He watched the man put cement on flat boards the bricklayers used. When the wheel barrow was empty he said "Put mud on all the bricklayers mortar boards and keep them full."

The man walked off picking up his trowel. "I'm Joe Acker the forman. If you work out the pay is five dollars a week. If you do good, I'll give you a two dollar raise next week."

John took the wheelbarrow back to the box and filled it with mortar. He went to each mortar board filling it. When the wheelbarrow was empty he went back and began making the cement as he was shown.

When John returned Joe looked at the mortar as John shoveled it on the board. It was the same as he had mixed it.

He did not smile. "Everytime, not sometime, but everytime the mortar is to be like this"

John stayed busy the rest of the day mixing mortar. It was hard work and he was tired when Joe said "No more mud."

He washed the box, wheelbarrow, shovel and hoe as Joe supervised. He walked to Ivy's boarding house tired.

John was up early each day. Ivy packed him lunch in a tin lunchbox. At the end of the week he was paid seven dollars. He was glad when he was able to pay Ivy for his room and board. Each night after dinner he sat outside with Ivy on the porch. Most of the men would leave going to the saloon, or visit a brothel. He soon fell into a routine of working at mixing cement for the bricklayers who were building a bank. It was the first brick building in Guthrie.

He would help Ivy do the dishes then they would sit out on the front porch in the cool evenings. John would read the newspapers of how Guthrie was growing. It was the capital of the new territory. He read of the Indians in the west who were a problem for settlers. The bandits were also a problem in the Indian Territory. Since Indian Territory was not a state and was considered a sovereign state for the Inidans. Many bandits would commit a crime in Kansas, Missouri, Texas or another state and flee to Indian Territory. The authorities in the states did not have jurisdiction and would have to contact the Federal Court in Little Rock Arkansas for a Marshal to go in and retrieve the desperado.

The warm summer days would pass as John worked on the new brick bank. One evening as he stood up from his chair on the porch Ivy looked at him smiling. She reached up with her small slender hand. He grasped it gently, helping her up. She stood up gracefully. She stepped close to him, putting her arms around his neck. She moved close to him, kissing him. John was surprised. Ivy stepped back, taking his hand. She walked toward the door glancing back at him. Inside the house She held his hand as she walked toward the staircase. Neither spoke as they walked up the stairs. Ivy walked to her door, opening it walking inside as John followed her holding her hand. His heart was beating fast as she shut the door behind him and stepped closer to him. His arms were around her slim waist. He felt her slender strong arms around his neck, her lips pressing against his. Breaking the embrace She stepped back and unbuttoned her dress.

Chapter XIII

The days became cooler as the last brick of the new bank was laid. Joe said he was going back to Texas with the colder weather setting in. Bricks could not be laid in the winter months since the mortar would freeze. John walked back to the boarding house now jobless. He would look for something and hoped he would find a job soon.

He was sitting on the front porch in the early evening as he watched a man tie up his horse and walk up the sidewalk toward the house. He had a badge on his vest and had a pistol on his hip. He stopped and looked at the men. He removed his hat looking at Ivy. "Good evening mam."

Ivy smiled and nodded at the Marshal. He put on his hat and looked at the group of men sitting on the porch.

"I'm Marshall Bill Thilghman. I'm looking for men to ride with me on a posse. We'll be going after the Doolin gang."

The men sat quietly. They had all heard of the desperados. The Doolin gang had robbed banks and trains. They were known as the wild bunch. All of the men in the Doolin gang were hard men.

John sat up, "I'll ride with you Marshall."

Ivy looked at John. "I don't think that is a good idea John. These men are hardened criminals."

"Meet me at the Sheriff's office at eight in the morning." He looked at the men sitting quietly. "Anyone else?" No one spoke. Marshall Tilghman turned and walked back toward his horse.

The following morning John walked to the sheriff's office where he saw a group of men standing. Marshall Tilghman walked toward him. "Do you have a horse?"

"No," John answered.

"How 'bout a gun?"

"No," he answered.

"Well this ain't no picnic we're goin on." A big man in a large floppy hat said grinning.

Marshall Tilghman walked inside the sheriff's office. He later walked out with a shotgun and shells. He handed the shotgun and shells to John.

"We'll get you a horse at the livery stable.

The group stopped at the livery stable where a horse was brought out. John put his clothes in a saddle bag and the shotgun in a scabbard on the saddle, tying his blanket onto the back of the saddle. He mounted the horse and followed the men out of town heading east.

The seven men rode east most of the day. None of them spoke. Marshall Tilghman stopped after several hours resting his horse near a creek;

"Where are we going, Marshall," a man in a derby hat asked."

"Ingalls, that's where the Doolin gang is holed up. They will put up a fight so we will need to be careful."

That evening the men stopped as it began to get dark. They removed their saddles and each man rubbed their horses down, tying them to a stake so they could rest and feed.

"Why we stopping here? We could spend the night in Stillwater in a hotel. I'm sure the Government could afford to put us up for the night." Jack Chambers, who was older, said frowning.

Marshall Tilghman did not look up as he put more wood on the fire.

"A posse going into Stillwater would tip off the wild bunch. They have low life friends I'm sure that would warn them. No, we'll spend the night here on Council Creek then in the morning catch them while they are asleep."

It made sense to John. He removed his blanket from the back of the saddle and spread it on the ground. He sat quietly as the coffee pot boiled. Marshall Tilghman removed a bag from his saddle bags and reaching in took out long strips of beef jerky. He handed each man two strips of jerky. When the coffee was done each man poured the strong smelling thick liquid in their tin cups and sat quietly sipping their coffee and eating the dry hard jerky.

A big man looked at John grinning showing his yellow teeth.

"I suppose you would rather be with the widder woman than out here in the cold. She keep you warm at night?"

John looked at the man who he had heard called Pete. He nodded as he looked at the big ugly man. "Maybe you should have stayed in town with the sewing circle. That way you could keep up with the gossip."

The man did not smile. He stared hard at John. "What's that supposed to mean?"

"All right boys, we can save the fighting for tomorrow. We don't need to be fighting among ourselves." Marshall Tilghman said looking over his cup he held close to his mouth.

"Perhaps we can sing a hymn? Would you like that Pete? Would you like to sing a Sunday school hymn?" John asked seriously.

Pete did not smile as the other men snickered. "Maybe you can tell us a story from Sunday school Pete." John said as he taunted the big man.

"Maybe I'll just give you a whuppin'." Pete said growling low.

"Whip, not whuppin, that would be more correct, you Ignoramus." John said, staring at the big ugly man.

THE MEN SAT NERVOUSLY knowing Pete Sanders was a mean man.

"In case you're wondering, your name in Latin is actually extremous smallous genatelliaous. Just thought you would want to know. It might be a small thing that comes up in your sewing circle."

Pete sat his cup down and began to rise.

"Sit down!" Marshall Tilghman barked. "I think we should turn in for the night." he looked at John glaring at him. John laid down on his blanket as did the other men.

John woke up the following morning in the dark when Marshall Tighlman kicked his feet with his boot. The men all rose stiff from sleeping on the hard ground. The night had been cold and the blanket was little comfort. The men sat quiet as they drank the strong black coffee.

When they finished the coffee, the fire was put out and the horses saddled. It was still dark as the posse made its way toward the small town of Ingalls. They did not go through Ingalls but skirted the town heading for a small farm on the outskirts.

Marshall Tilghman positioned the men around the house. The sun was rising as a man stepped out of the house. Tilghman yelled "throw up you're hands!"

The man ran for the house as the posse fired. The men inside responded as lead was now flying thick in the air. The outlaws were able to shoot their way out the back door running for their horses. John followed Marshall Tilghman loading the double barreled shotgun as they ran for the back.

The outlaws were on their horses riding hard as the posse fired. One outlaw was surrounded. He had run out of ammunition. John stepped toward him with the shotgun saying "drop the rifle."

The man slowly lowered the rifle. Marshal Tilghman walked up to him putting on heavy shackles. He stared at the man.

"Roy Daugherty, goes by Arkansas Tom Jones." He grasped the outlaws arm walking him to a horse. He placed the man on a horse.

Three of the men in the posse had been killed. Marshall Tilghman sighing heavily. He looked at the men laying across the saddles who had died in the battle.

"Pete take Roy to Guthrie with the three dead men. Sheriff Thomas will see their families are notified. You two come with me."

The posse rode throughout the day towards Stillwater. They stopped on the outskirts of town that evening. The three men walked into a large two story house that was well furnished entering through the back door. Marshall Tilghman said to a lady working in the kitchen.

"Tell Sadie to come in here alone."

The woman walked out quickly. A small woman in a low cut dress walked into the kitchen. She did not smile as she saw the heavily armed men. Marshall Tilghman stepped up to her.

"I know the wild bunch is here. Tell me where they are." The woman had a hard look. She did not answer as she glared at the Marshall. His eyes narrowed. "If we go in looking for them, we will go in shooting."

Sadie said in a low voice. "Two are playing poker in the east room. The other is in room four."

The Marshall pointed to John and Jack, "go into the east room and hold the men until I come down. Don't shoot unless you have to. We only want the two. I don't want anyone else to die."

John followed Marshall Tilghman out of the door and immediately went to the room on the far east side of the building. He walked in with Jack behind him pointing the shotgun at the five men playing cards. They all looked surprised.

"Put your hands on the table and no one moves." The men slowly put their hands on the table looking at the double barreled shotgun and a Winchester rifle pointed at them.

Marshall Tilghman walked up the stairs quickly, pulling his colt pistol, opening the door and walking inside. The man in bed with a woman was surprised,

"You know my name," he said quietly. "Step out of bed and put your pants on." The man slowly slid out of bed putting his pants and boots on. Marshall Tilghman tipped his hat to the woman in bed. "Evening Mam."

He walked the outlaw out of the room and down the steps. They walked into the room where John and Jack stood watching the men at the poker table. Marshall Tilghman pointed to two men. "Stand up with your hands high."

The two men slowly stood up. John removed their pistols from their holsters. He and Jack marched the men out of the room. Marshall Tilghman said as he left.

"Gentlemen have a good evening."

The outlaws were taken to the Stillwater jail.

Chapter XIV

John and Jack were up early the following day. They followed Marshall Tilghman to the Stillwater Jail. The outlaws were removed and shackles placed on their wrists and ankles.

Marshall Tilghaman with the outlaws in the back of a wagon with John and Jack headed for the train station. When they arrived at the train depot the outlaws sat on a wooden bench against the wall of the train station. Marshall Tilghman purchased tickets for the group to travel to Guthrie. John was glad to be riding the train as his legs were sore.

The train did not leave until two in the afternoon. All they could do was wait. Marshall Tilghman left John and Jack with the outlaws to pursue Bill Doolin.

When the train arrived in Stillwater the outlaws were herded aboard the train bound for Guthrie. It would take two hours to reach their destination and home.

The jail in Guthrie was built with money from private investors. The jail was leased back to the federal Government to hold outlaws. The businessmen bragged how their jail was escape proof. The men were turned over to the Sheriff's office. They were checked into the jail. John and Jack shook hands and headed for home.

John arrived at the boarding house seeing Ivy sitting in a rocking chair knitting. She looked up seeing John walk into the room. She stood up walking quickly to John putting her arms around his neck kissing him. She laid her head on his chest saying softly, "I've missed you. I was so worried that something would happen." She looked at him with moist eyes. "I'm glad you're home John."

The next evening Ivy placed a big pot of beans with fried potatoes and cornbread on the table telling the men to help themselves. She instructed them to leave the bowls in the sink and she would wash them later. She smiled, "John is taking me out."

The restaurant was nice, and crowded. Ivy had on a nice dress she only wore on special occasions. They sat quietly talking and smiling as they enjoyed the evening. When supper was finished they walked to the opera house where a band was performing. When the concert ended they walked under the full moon on a cold evening. The stars were shining as John held Ivey's hand. Their boots echoed off the wooden sidewalks as they walked.

John stopped as he saw Pete sitting in an old wooden chair outside a saloon. Pete stood up scowling at John. "I'm gonna beat you to death, smart mouth."

"Now Pete I thought we were friends. I was hoping you would come to Sunday School with me tomorrow."

Pete was unsteady on his feet. He stepped forward as John moved Ivy behind him. He dropped her hand and stepped toward the big man in front of him. Pete swung wildly missing John's head as he ducked. John with his fist hit Pete hard in the stomach. The air seemed to leave the big man's body as he doubled over. John brought up his fist striking Pete under the chin. Pete staggered back falling off the sidewalk onto the hard dusty ground.

John turned, taking Ivy's small hand. "Shall we continue home my dear."

She did not speak as she looked at John then to the big man laying on the ground. She squeezed his hand and walked close to John.

A few days later John was able to find a Job at the Sentinel, one of the newspapers in Guthrie. He was able to read so he was hired as a type setter. He had to adjust to the type being placed in the rack of the printing press backwards. It was confusing at first but after working for a week at the Sentinel he soon had the hang of the press. When the type was set he would take a large brush and dip it in black ink spreading it over the iron letters. Then load the printer with paper, start the machine and watch as the printing press moved quickly pressing the paper against the letters. He would continually spread more ink so the writing on the page was clear. He enjoyed the job and liked the people he worked with. It was at the paper he learned of Marshall Tilghman bringing in Bill Doolin. Weeks later Doolin and fourteen other men would break out of the escape proof jail. They would grab the jailer who had neglected to lock the outside door behind him as he entered the cell areas. They would all run for the exits. All of the men would eventually be caught. Bill Dooling would be tracked to Pauls Valley where his in- laws lived. Sheriff Heck Thomas, Marshall Tilghman with a posse would kill the outlaw after a gunfight.

John had settled in to Guthrie and enjoyed the frontier town. The town was growing and talk of a new state was the rumor in town. He liked being with Ivy and began attending church with her.

She would smile shyly saying "it would be more appropriate if they were not living in sin, and a child should have a Father and Mother."

John smiled, saying "I agree."

The cold winter would soon give up its icy grip as the green grass and small buds on the trees could be seen. Spring time was a welcomed sight.

John sat up in bed feeling the pain shoot through his head. He stepped out of bed holding his head. He was in pain as he dropped to his knees. His body began to shake, and soon he was gone.

Josh Baker sat up suddenly as he saw the red light blinking. He pushed the red button alerting the team a jump was happening. Dr. Wright ran into the control room with a concerned look on her face. She looked at the computer screen then looked at the empty room through the glass. She waited anxious, barely breathing. The light went off and nothing more happened. Joanne was surprised, expecting to see Brian in the clean sanitized room.

"What happened?" William Shakely asked nervously.

"I'm not sure Brian should be here right now."

"He's jumped into the future!" Beth said excitedly.

"What! I thought you said he was going to stop here! What is going on Doctor Wright?"

William Shakley yelled.

Joanne ignored him and moving Josh away from the computer began typing furiously. She did not look up as her fingers flew across the computer screen.

"We will get him back." She said as she worked furiously.

William Shakley turned and walked out of the control room angrily. Joanne looked at Beth who was also working on her computer.

"Call everyone in. We need to get Brian back."

Beth looked up as Josh was on the phone calling all the men and women who worked in the lab.

"He may keep jumping." Beth said quietly.

"No, we will get him back," Joanne said nervously.

Chapter XV

He opened his eyes in the brightly lit room. It happened again, he thought. He was no longer in Ivy's bed. He didn't know where he was or even when. He felt depression crawling over him. He didn't care any more. He just wanted all this insanity to stop.

His eyes adjusted to the bright room. He saw a woman standing at the end of the bed. She was wearing a white coat. His memory raced as the sight looked familiar. He had dreams of men and women in white coats. She was pretty. He thought how she looked somewhat like Ivy.

She did not smile as she looked at him. "What is your name? What Cooperation do you work for?"

She was matter of fact with no emotion.

"I don't know. I don't remember anything."

Her eyebrow raised slightly as her voice was also elevated. "You don't know? You won't tell because you're a spy."

"Spy, why do you think I'm a spy? Who are you, and where am I?" the man asked, becoming angry.

The woman stood quiet. She walked from the back of the bed to the side, staying away not getting too close. "Why do you have a chip in your head that is over a hundred and fifty years old?"

"What chip are you talking about? I don't have a chip in my head."

The woman watched the man. She was confused. "Why don't you have a chip in your cerebral cortex?" she asked more out of curiosity.

He was tired and did not know what this woman was talking about. Chip? What did she mean with a chip in his head?

"Where am I?" he asked wearily.

The woman was quiet. "You're in the Northwest conglomerate Headquarters."

"What is that?" he asked.

She thought he was playing dumb. She stood quiet looking at the strange man who had been brought into the infirmary. He had been found in the grass on the front lawn. He was naked. She was surprised when there was no identifying chip in his head. All the corporations had chips implanted in their people. The small chips imbed in the cerebral cortex helped corporations track their people. It was also useful if a person was out of control to send a calming message to the individual. It didn't always work. The chip could not be used to control people. It was used for tracking. She thought it odd he could be found inside the most secure building complex on the planet. He was odd.

"What city is this and what is the date?"

"Chicago." She said softly. She was not sure why he was asking about the date.

"Illinois, I'm in Illinois." He said surprised.

The woman was surprised, there had not been states for over eighty years. Corporations now run the world. The state Governments had been replaced when the debt was so large Corporations bought the Government. There had been little resistance since the Government was so corrupt; only a few elite people were benefiting as the majority of the world population lived in deplorable conditions. The Corporations had done away with Governments and now all people worked for a corporation. It was now more fair with all people employed. There were of course wars from time to time when a Corporation tried to take over another. Spying on corporations was a constant threat. Corporate espionage where secrets were stolen concerned all the companies. Four big Corporations ran the world.

The Americorp which ran all of what was Canada, United States and South America. The Asian Corporation which ran China, Korea,

Japan and the Philippines. European Alliance Corporation which ran all of Europe, and the Russian Corporation which ran Russia and the remainder of the countries.

She stood quiet watching the man as he had fallen asleep. She walked on tip toes and slowly scanned him. She would run tests and determine who he was.

Walking out of the room she stopped seeing the guard.

"He woke up briefly but he is asleep. You should notify the Chief."

"The young man was staring at the pretty Doctor.

"Okay, Mam, yes I'll contact the chief."

She smiled at him as she walked off.

Sydney Martin walked into the conference room sitting down next to her boss Raymond Turner. She leaned over saying "he woke up."

Ray started to speak when the door opened and the Director walked in sitting down at the end of the long table. He opened his folder studying the agenda when he heard "Director, Doctor Martin has information you need to hear sir."

He looked up closing the folder. "Doctor Martin enlighten us please."

Sydney looked directly at Director Mahoney. "The man in the infirmary woke up."

All eyes were now on Sydney. "He says he doesn't know his name."

"Well of course he would say that. He's obviously a spy." Sydney was interrupted by Twila Allen. She was Deputy Director of Research and Development, including Security.

"Why don't you allow Doctor Martin to finish before you interrupt Twila." Ray said curtly.

TWILA'S EYES NARROWED as she leaned forward. Before she could speak, Director Mahoney said "Continue Doctor Martin."

Sydney hesitated as the tension in the room was now heavy.

"The man claims to have no memory. He..."

"He's lying! I'll have Chief Powell speak to him." Twila interrupted her again."

"I've notified Chief Powell." Sydney said flatly.

"Perhaps you should go interview the man Twila. It's obvious you don't want to hear what Doctor Martin has to report." Director Mahoney said, staring at Twila.

She returned his stare without blinking.

"Perhaps I've missed something. I am still the Director of Americorp. Was there a change and I was not notified?"

"You're still Director." Twila said flatly.

"Okay then, stop interrupting. The rest of us would like to hear what Doctor Martin has to report."

Twila sat back fuming. She did not like to be challenged by anyone. She was the youngest person appointed Deputy Director in the history of the company. She was a driven woman and made things happen. She could be brutal when dealing with any staff member.

Syndey took a breath and continued. "He is a strange individual. I have never seen anyone like him. He asked where he was. I told him Chicago."

"That was a Mistake." Twila said, staring at Sydney."

"Why?" Raymond asked. What difference does it make?"

Twila's eyes blazed with fury.

"Are you going to continue to interrupt my meeting?" The Director asked. Twila stared at him without speaking. "I called the meeting, therefore, it is my meeting. Interrupt again and you will be escorted out of the building. Do you understand Twila?"

"I understand sir." she said flatly.

"The man stated Illinois, I'm in Illinois." Sydney said as the room sat stunned. No one spoke. The Director looked at Twila who sat quiet.

Everyone in the room was surprised. No one could even remember states, and it was only in history classes they were talked of. The Director sat back as he watched Sydney.

She continued. "I was surprised by his response. I have been analyzing the man for two days while he slept. He does not have a chip in his cerebral cortex. It appears he has never had one implanted. He does have a chip." Sydney hesitated choosing her words carefully. "He has a chip that is over a hundred and fifty years old implanted in the back of his brain in the temporal region, connected to the spinal column and pituitary gland. I asked him about the chip and he responded "what chip? I don't have a chip in my head.""

The men and women in the room sat stunned. The Director leaned forward in his chair. "How is that even possible?"

"It's not." Twila blurted out.

"How do you know Twila? Did you scan the man, or examine him?" Ray said, raising his voice.

Twila leaned forward. "I don't have to. I know it is not remotely possible."

Ray sat back in his chair. "Well I guess that's it. Let's cancel the meeting and go back to work. Twila knows for a fact without speaking to the man or examining him. Doctor Martin is mistaken. The most gifted Doctor and scientist we have and Twila knows best!"

Twila Allen was on her feet. "Watch your mouth Ray! I won't be talked to this way from you."

"Enough! The Director rose slowly glaring at the group. He looked at Twila. "Sit down!"

Twila stared at the older man. She sat down furious, staring at Ray. He took a breath and sat down. "Doctor Martin, how is this possible?"

Sydney wanted to run out of the room. The tension in the room was intense. She swallowed and said quietly. "I don't know Director. I only have preliminary data. I need to do a deep scan and spend more comprehensive time on this subject. Anything I say will be conjecture."

"When can you have a more detailed report?" The Director asked calmly.

"Two weeks."

"I can have it done in a week." Twila said sarcastically.

"It's not your area, Twila." Ray said sharply.

"He's right." The Director said, looking at Twila. He looked back at Sydney. "Can you remove the chip?"

"I can't say for sure. I don't want to risk damaging it. I have never seen a chip like this. I'm not sure how it is attached. I don't want to kill the man."

The room was quiet. No one spoke as they waited for the Director.

"Okay, Doctor Martin, I would like a report on your progress in two weeks." He stood up saying, "we will continue the meeting after lunch."

The rest of the people in the room stood up leaving as the Director walked into his office. He said, "Twila step in my office."

Twila sat across from the Director's desk. "I believe I made a mistake promoting you Twila. The Chief of Staff position is open. I believe it would be best if you take that position."

"I was Chief of Staff. Director I know I can be irritating at times but I get things done for you."

"No, what you do is get things done for you. It is always about you first."

"I'm sorry Director."

They sat silently looking at each other.

After a while the Director said "I do not want you to interrupt me in my meetings. You have a tendency to try and take over. You are the most hated Deputy Director in the company. You are ambitious to the point of being dangerous."

"I'm sorry, Director. I am ambitious, but I am learning from you."

He sat back as he looked at her. "You need to get along with other Department Heads. That means you don't run their areas. If you don't show some teamwork you will be gone by next quarter."

Twila did not smile as she stood up and walked out of the Directors office.

Chapter XVI

Sydney walked to her office and sat down. She leaned back in her chair thinking how much she hated going to the Directors meetings. It was hell every time. The Deputy Directors were always fighting and attempting to place themselves over the others. Twila Allan was the worst. She was a cut throat woman whose only ambition was to be Director. She shook her head thinking of how terrible it would be with that witch in charge.

She stood up walking out of her office. She rode the elevator to the ground floor then walked out into the beautiful lobby. Once outside she walked down the marble steps to the street. She waited for the trolly as it slowly hovered by. She stepped on seeing it was half full.

Sydney was lost in her thoughts as she looked at the beautiful landscape of the compound. When the trolly slowed at the back of the compound several people stepped off the trolly. Sydney also stepped off the trolly. Sydney followed the small group to one of the maintenance buildings where repair technicians were working. It was an expansive building used as a warehouse.

Inside the building She walked past work tables with men and women working on different machines. She did not look at them as she made her way to the back where the freight elevator was located.

Sidney stepped onto the dirty floor of the huge elevator. Pushing the button to the basement she waited impatiently as the old elevator used for hauling up equipment, and other supplies moved slowly down.

When the freight elevator stopped she stepped out into the dusty basement. She walked past rows of materials and equipment on pallets stacked higher than her head.

In the far back of the basement in the right corner next to the bathroom was an office with the door opened. She could hear loud music playing and saw Bandy sitting at a desk. He was wearing a multi-colored tee shirt, dark pants with the legs rolled up to his knees, wearing long socks that were stripped. His red hair was sticking straight up with a bandanna on.

"Hey Bandy!" Sydney shouted loudly over the blaring music.

Bandy looked up, his blue eyes looking through large round glasses.

He grinned "Hey Syd, welcome to the dungeon!" He reached over, turning down the music. "What brings you slumming Syd?"

Sydney smiled sitting down. "I need your help."

"We gonna take out the she-devil?"

No, Bandy and don't say that. I have a unique problem and you are the only one who can help me."

Bandy sat the old computer hard drive down. He was an outcast that Twila had banished to the basement. No one asked him for help or even talked to him. Sydney was his best friend and had kept him from being exiled to the far reaches of the company when he embarrassed Twila Allen.

He was intrigued. "Okay what's up?"

Sydney sat back. "I need you to look at a chip that is over a hundred and fifty years old. I don't know the brand, maker or what it is composed of. I'm afraid it will be damaged if it is not handled right. You know more about the old computers and systems than anyone on the planet. I need your help."

Bandy was sitting up hanging on every word. He had a passion for the old computer systems and had collected old computers, jump drives, disc's, and chips.

"You say over a hundred and fifty years old? That's great! I have some stuff older than that. Let me see it and I will help you with this mystery."

"I don't have it with me. It is in the brain of a man in the hospital. The chip is in a place that is sensitive. If I remove it I could kill the man, or damage the chip where it can not be read."

Bandy sat back staring at Sydney. "The chip is implanted in a man. What is he two hundred years old?"

"No thirty eight according to his DNA scan."

Bandy shook his head. "Who is this guy? And is he with the company?"

"I don't know Bandy. He says he has no memory. He was found two days ago on the front lawn naked."

"So what is it you want me to do?"

"I want you to do what you do. Scan the chip and tell me what it is. Where it is from. Who made it? And I want you to do this without taking it out."

Bandy laughed. "Do you want me to open a direct line to God so you can talk to him?"

Sydney did not smile. "I don't like it when you mock the Lord." She stood up. "I'll find someone else to help me." She turned quickly walking away.

"I'm sorry Syd. Hey, what you're asking is not going to be easy. You know I'm your guy. Who else are you gonna get?"

"That's why I came to you, Bandy. You are the only one who can help me. But if you're just going to be a smart alec then I'll find someone else."

"No, I want to help. It's just this is the craziest thing I've ever heard of, and trust me I know crazy."

Sydney stopped at the door. "Okay Bandy, meet me in the front lobby of headquarters tomorrow at nine. Wear your uniform and keep your equipment minimal." She started to leave then turned around. "Bandy don't talk. Please be quiet and don't say anything."

Bandy smiled, "Got ya."

The ride in the tube that stretched across the city was quiet. The small train was quiet as it glided quickly inside the transparent tube. Sydney looked at the fading sunlight admiring the beautiful colors of the sitting sun. She was troubled but felt more relaxed as she saw her neighborhood. When the train stopped Sydney stepped out of the tube and walked to her house. She enjoyed the walk which was two blocks. The old elm trees lining the streets were beautiful. Arriving at her home She saw walkin in, her family sitting at the table eating. Her daughter jumped up running to her "Mommy!"

Sydney hugged the excited child. Who began to tell her of school. A robot walked up "now Caroline you have not finished your supper."

She ignored him as they walked to the table. The robot brought a plate of food to Sydney. "I kept it warm for you Doctor Martin."

"Thank you Simon." Sydney began eating as Caroline talked of going to art class while in school.

"You have not eaten your beans Caroline." Simon said as he fed Cory Sydney's son who was one.

"I only eat beans Papa brings me." Caroline said, looking at her plate.

"Jelly beans are not a vegetable." Simon said.

"Caroline you need to eat your beans."Sydney said looking at her daughter. "Or you wont get any desert. "

"So how was your day honey?" Her husband Jacob, asked?

"I had to go to the Directors Department Head meeting."

Jacob raised his eyebrows. "Your latest project I presume?"

"Yes, it was painful."

When supper was finished. The family gathered in the living room to spend time together. Carolyn ran to her room and came back showing a picture she had drawn in art class. Sydney was impressed as she looked at the drawing. It was good for a five year old.

"The teacher read a book of people who lived in caves. It was a long time ago. Teacher said to draw a picture of the people."

Jacob looked over Sydney's shoulder "that's good Caroline, did Simon help you?"

"No, he didn't. I drew it myself."

Jacob smiled as he looked at the picture of a woman on a rock with a big tiger looking up at her. "Is that mommy on the rock?" he asked.

"Yes and the tiger's name is Simon."

"I told her that it was not appropriate." Simon said he stood at the back of the room.

When the children were in bed Sydney asked "Jacob I know you teach computers and systems at the University. Is it possible to place a chip that is over a hundred and fifty years old in a person."

He was surprised at the question. "I guess I would ask why you would want too."

"Well then, why would a chip that old be in a person?" Sydney asked.

Jacob thought for a while. "I suppose if the chip was of a better quality, it could be used," he thought for a while. "Perhaps there is information on the chip that the person's brain could integrate with to show a difference in ability. I really don't know. Why do you ask?"

Sydney needed to be careful. Jacob was her husband but the information was sensitive. "Could you read the chip without taking it out?"

"No, I would have to have the chip. You would need an old computer system that was compatible to read it. I'm not sure." Jacob was now curious.

"I have a man in the hospital who has a chip in his head that is old. It is in the Temporal area of the brain next to the stem. I asked Bandy to help me read it."

Jacob sat quiet. "Rex Bandicardin, You're talking about Rex? The man was banished for humiliating Twila Allen."

"Yes. He knows more about the old computers than anyone."

"Yes and he is a genius. A weirdo, strange little man who proved Twila Allen was making up data on her reports. You know she eats her enemies when she kills them."

"I know he is not liked by many. But do you think he can scan a chip without it being removed."

"Probably, he's the only person who could. He however is considered a plague."

Sydney was quiet. "He's my friend Jacob. Please don't be so mean. I grew up with Bandy. I..." She trailed off as the tears came.

Jacob walked over sitting next to her. He put his arm around her.

"Sydney, you have to be careful. Rex Bandicardin is considered enemy number one. Twila Allen is mean and vindictive."

"I know." She whispered.

Chapter XVII

Sydney saw Bandy standing on the first landing of the steps as she walked toward headquarters. He was wearing brown slacks and a white starched shirt. His hair was combed and he had on shoes. He looked like any other tech.

She smiled, "Good morning Bandy."

He smiled "Good morning Sydney.

They walked together up the steps to the big doors of the building. Neither spoke as they walked across the large lobby area to the elevators. The elevator was full of staff each getting off on different floors. When the light read five they both stepped off. The elevator would continue up to the one hundred and twentieth floor.

Sydney was nervous as she walked up to the door with the young security officer standing guard. He smiled at Sydney as she smiled back, She opened the door walking inside followed by Bandy. They saw the man was awake. He was eating breakfast.

He looked at them as he continued to eat.

"I would like to take a shower."

"Okay, when we finish our exam I will ask the officer to escort you to the shower."

"What kind of exam? I hope you don't want to probe me in sensitive places?"

"Would you like to be probed?" Bandy asked.

"Would you like me to beat you to death?" The man in bed said without smiling.

"No, I would not like that." Bandy said, dropping his smile.

Sydney said as she approached the bed. "I need you to stand up. There will be no probing. It will be noninvasive."

The man stood up wearing only pajama bottoms.

"I need you to remove all your clothes." Sydney said as she looked at her equipment.

"We don't know each other that well honey."

"You need to get naked." Sydney said not smiling.

He removed his pajama bottoms. Sydney could see numerous scars and burns on his body. She began to scan him with her hand held scanner. It was slow as the beams of light pulsated.

She was standing close to him when she asked "How did you get the scars and burns? There are old fractures that have healed."

"In battle."

"What kind of battle? Sydney asked as she reached up to scan his head.

"The kind of battles where scars and burns occur." He said leaning close to her face.

She saw he was nice looking. Sydney did not move back. She walked slowly around him.

When she finished the scanning she said "you can get dressed."

He picked up his pajamas and put them on.

Bandy walked to him. "Have a seat sir."

He sat in a chair as the smaller man reached in his briefcase taking out a machine.

"What's that?"

Bandy smiled. "It will scan the inside of your head to see if there is anything in between your ears."

"You the court jester?" The man said as he turned to look at Bandy.

"Yeah, a banished jester."

Bandy placed a cap with small silver sensors on the man's head. A small scanner was placed on the cap. He felt the vibration as the machine moved slowly around his head. After a short while Bandy stepped back. "I'm finished," He picked up the machine placing it in his small bag. "I need to read it." He looked at Sydney, " Are you going to put me in a closet?"

"I should?" Sydney said as she walked to the door.

When they left the room, the officer stepped in saying to the man "come with me and you can have a shower. Doctor Martin says you asked for one."

"How about a shave and a haircut?"

"Sure." The officer said, smiling.

Sydney shut the office door and plugged in the scanner into her computer. Bandy removed an old laptop computer and plugged in his scanner as well. They both sat quietly looking at the data.

Sydney said "Bandy come here look at this."

He walked over peering into the large computer screen. Sydney pointed to the back of the skull. "Here in the Temporal region you can see the chip. It is connected to the stem of the central nervous system. " She looked confused saying "see this thin wire, it appears to be attached to the optic nerve."

Bandy sat down as he stared at the brain. "I can't be certain. I will need to study the information, but I don't think that is a wire. It is called coax which carries impulses of light. This chip may be recording what the man sees." He pointed to a small bump on the wire. "That may be a camera." He sat back. looking at the brain. "He could have information which includes what he sees as well as recording conversations that are being stored on the chip. I remember decoding Asian chips that did the same. They were smaller and more sophisticated." he pointed to the stem of the spinal column.

"I don't know what this is. I've never seen anything like this. It appears to be some kind of mechanism"

Bandy stood up walking to his computer looking at the data. After a while he looked up. "It is gonna take me a while. I have to admit I have no idea what all this wiring and that mechanism is for. It is beyond my knowledge. I mean if this is one hundred and fifty years old, it is more sophisticated than I thought possible for the time. I don't know what it could be."

Sydney studied the man's skeleton. She was confused finding a thin wire running the length of his skeleton. Bandy did not know what it was either. The man seemed to be in good physical shape. He did not have any diseases or problems. She checked his blood then sent it to the mainframe in order to analyze his DNA. She hoped the Artificial Intelligence in the powerful computer could give her information on who the mystery man was. Bandy left saying he was heading for the dungeon to study information from the chip.

Early in the afternoon the door opened as Raymond stepped inside. He walked over to a chair and sat down. Sydney was looking at her computer. She looked at him.

"Any developments on the mystery man in the hospital?"

"Yes a lot of developments actually. The problem is they raise more questions." She pointed to the picture on the screen. "You can see the chip in the Temporal Region of his brain. There is a wire that runs to the octave nerve. Also this small connection to his pituitary gland. The wire runs the length of his skeleton and is connected to a mechanism." She sat back "I have no idea how it works or the purpose."

"Perhaps Rex Bandicardin can help."Sydney turned and looked at him. Ray leaned forward. "I received a visit from Twila Allan. She was not pleased when the scanners picked up Rex entering the building. Also when he was scanned going into the room of our mystery man. She made it clear he was never to enter the building ever."

Sydney was silent as she sat listening.

She sat up slowly, "I needed an expert on old computer systems to read the chip. I do not believe it can be removed without damaging it or killing the man. Bandy knows more of the old computers and chips than anyone on the planet."

"I realize that." Ray said standing up. "I told Twila she needed to stay out of my business. She was not happy. "I will support you Sydney, but you need to tread carefully."

"I understand." She almost whispered.

Sydney studied the information carefully of the strange chip and wiring inside the man. She began to understand how the strange system that seemed simple and antiquated was in fact very sophisticated. She was surprised that the computer technicians of that era were so complex.

She was studying the data when she was notified the DNA results of the man were complete. She opened the file and was shocked to see the man was related to her. She looked in awe at the line of descendants realizing the gap of over three hundred years. She had descendants on her grandmother's side of her family going back to Ivy Green from Guthrie Oklahoma. She sat back thinking how her family had lived in Oklahoma for generations. She had cousins that still lived there. Her cousins were listed on a separate branch. They only shared DNA from her maternal side of the family. Her great great great grandfather was the man in the hospital room. His name was listed as John Smith. He was only a few years older than her.

Sydney could see a strange break in the tree she could not explain. A hundred and fifty years showed the man's name Brian White. He seemed to be the last of his people. She traced the man's history back to England, Scotland, Ireland, and Germany.

She was again surprised to see another branch that listed her husband Jacob. He had DNA listed as Denisovan. They were a human ancestor that predated Neanderthol.

Sydney sat back as she looked at the fragmented family tree. It was the strangest thing she had ever seen. She had studied genealogy while at the university. It was a difficult and complex class. She had done well and had often been called to help unravel issues with family ancestry. This was something that did not make sense. It showed ancestry going back thousands of years. How could this man's DNA be linked to a Denisovan woman? It was not possible for him to have a son with her. She was confused at how he also had a daughter with a woman in 1896. The man was born in the year 2022. There must be a mistake. The computer must have had a glitch.

When Sydney arrived at home she asked Simon to read the data and give his impressions. Simon was one of the most sophisticated robots on the planet. His artificial intelligence was highly advanced. She spoke to Jacob about the results of the man's DNA. Jacob was stunned not knowing what to say. He was at a loss of words and could not comprehend the information.

Later that evening Simon sat in front of Sydney and Jacob in a chair facing them. He said "I have analyzed the data, Doctor Martin. It appears this man Bryan White was born in 2022 and is the father of a Denisovan child one hundred thousand years ago. He is also the father of a child from three hundred years ago. It is not logical how this is possible. The only explanation I can offer is that he has figured out how to travel in time."

"I do not believe that is possible Simon." Sydney said, wrinkling her brow.

"Theoretically it is possible, Doctor Martin. According To Albert Einstein it is possible to travel back in time according to his equations."

Chapter XVIII

Sydney was surprised as she walked off the elevator the following day. She had expected to see the young guard in front of the door. He was not at his post. She walked into the room seeing the bed was empty. The man was not there.

She walked quickly to the elevators and rode to the ground floor. She walked to the front desk. "Where is the man who was in room 505?"

The young man looked on his computer then said looking up.

"He was checked out by Chief Powell."

Sydney felt the anger and frustration as she thought how Twila Allen was making a power play for the strange man. She immediately called Raymond telling him she was going to the detention center. Ray said he would talk with the Director immediately.

Sydney walked into the detention center going to the desk Sergeant. She leaned forward saying "I want to see Chief Powell immediately. Tell him Doctor Martin is here to talk to him."

The man sat looking back at the beautiful woman who was obviously upset. He picked up the phone and called his Chief of Security.

A few minutes later Chief Powell and Twila Allen walked to the lobby.

"I want to see my patient. You have no right to remove him without my order of release."

"I have every right Doctor Martin..."

Sydney stepped up to Twila, interrupting her. "No, you do not! You have violated many regulations of the company by removing a patient that is under a doctor's care."

Twila was surprised and angry as Sydney continued. "You will return the patient under my care immediately Deputy Director Allan or I will bring charges against you and Chief Powell for this outrage"

"Go ahead." Twila said arrogantly.

Sydney stepped up to Chief Powell. He was a big man who was dark complected. "I assume you know the regulations of hospital security Chief. I need to see my patient now so I can examine him."

"Your request is denied!" Twila said loudly.

Sydney ignored her. "Chief are you going to deny patient care by denying his Doctor to see him?"

Chief Powell was nervous. He was well aware of the regulations of patient care. It was a fundamental rule of Americorp. People were always to be treated humanely.

"I will allow you to see your patient Doctor Martin. He is currently in a cell."

"You will not Chief! I will decide who sees this man!" Twila yelled.

"No mam you do not have the authority, nor does the Director. Policy is clear no one may deny a Doctor access to their patient. I'm sorry Mrs. Allen but the Doctor has the right under our regulations to see her patient."

Twila was stunned she believed her word was law, now Her Chief was disobeying her. "Are You diobaying my order Chief?"

"Yes Mam I am." Chief Powell said flatly.

Twila stormed out of the building.

Chief Powell escorted Sydney to the holding cells.

Sydney walked in hearing the door shut behind her. She saw Brian sitting on the edge of the bed. He looked up seeing the pretty Doctor.

"Are you here to break me out Doctor Martin?"

"I will get you out Brian. There is no way to break you out." The man looked at her curiously. She continued as she sat next to him. "How did you do it Brian. Please explain to me how you time travel? I'm sure the chip and strange mechanism in your body has something to do with it."

He was quiet as he stood up walking to the door. He stood for a long time looking into space. He finally turned to look at Sydney. "I have no idea. I do not have any memory. The only thing I know is that I woke up in a strange land and there were strange small people who lived in a cave. I stayed with them for some time then one night I had a severe pain in my head. I woke up and was in another land and time. It continues to happen. I don't know what is happening to me."

Sydney sat quietly on the hard bed listening intently. What he was saying made sense according to the data. It did not make sense logically. She stood up.

"You have no memory of who you are?"

"That's right. I cannot remember anything before I was in the wild country."

"Your name is Brian White. You were a soldier in the army special forces in the year 2040 until 2055. Then you suddenly vanished from the records. According to DNA you have a child from a Denisovan woman from a hundred thousand years ago. That son through you has hundreds of thousands of descendants related to him. You have a daughter from the old state of Oklahoma and thousands of descendants related to you. Including me. You are a time traveler."

Brian walked to the bed and sat down. It all made sense. He felt the regret of knowing Ela, and Ivy had been dead for many years. He was overwhelmed. He finally looked up. "It will happen again. I will wake up and I will be somewhere else."

"When? Can you tell me when it will happen again?"

"No, I don't know. I feel pain in my head then it happens."

Sydney sat talking to Brian for an hour then left the cell.

She walked into her office seeing Bandy sitting in a chair. He immediately jumped up running to her.

"I have something you have to see." He grasped her hand and ran to her desk. She saw his hand was shaking as his hands went across the computer keys. "This is from the chip I scanned.

The screen flickered then she saw a large open space that looked like a prairie. She saw wild animals roaming in the grassy plains. She watched as an arrow brought down a large rabbit. She saw the hide being cleaned. Sydney watched as fire was made from flint rocks. She saw a small woman running and a huge tiger chasing her. She sat stunned as she looked into the face of the woman who she knew was no doubt Denisovan, an ancient ancestor of Jacob. She blushed when she knew Brian was making love to her.

Bandy hit a key on the computer and she again saw Brian talking with men. She sat up as she looked into the face of Mary. She had been raised Christian and to see the face of the Mother of Jesus was awesome. The computer would continue to play different areas of the life Brian had lived. She saw the face of her fifth great grandmother. She looked like her Mother and grandmother.

When Bandy stopped the computer he said "I believe it is the Genesis Paradox. That was a program that created time travel and sent a man back in time. The project has always been considered theory. I don't believe it is a theory. This man is that same man from the Genesis Paradox."

Sydney's brain was racing as she listened to Bandy. She had studied the Genesis Paradox at the University. It was only a theory and could not be proved it had actually taken place. There was some circumstantial evidence but it was mostly speculation.

She stood up thinking "they actually did it." She turned to Bandy. "There must have been a mistake or they chose to come to the future. I don't know why they would take such a chance. Keep this quiet. Show it to no one. I have to speak to Ray."

Sydney rode the elevator to the one hundred twentieth floor. She stepped out going into the Directors office. Inside was the Director, Ray and Twila. She could feel the tension in the air. She sat down.

The Director said "we seem to have a conflict Doctor Martin."

"No sir, there is no conflict. Deputy Director Allen has removed a patient from the hospital without my knowledge or permission."

"There is nothing wrong with the man. He is healthy." Twila said arrogantly.

"That's not the point Twila. The man is under a doctor's care and security under your orders removed him!" Ray said, raising his voice.

Twila sat back glaring.

Sydney knew she was walking in a landmine area. She had two powerful Deputy Directors and the Director now looking at her. She took a deep breath. "I believe the man should be placed back into the hospital so more examinations can be completed. It is imperative he be returned."

The Director looked at Twila, "is there a reason you had the man removed from the hospital?"

"The man is healthy. The regulation is for only sick patients."

"That's not what the regulation says and you know it. The truth is you want to experiment on the man." Ray said not raising his voice.

Twila sat up "That is a lie!"

"Enough" the Director said, irritated. "The man is to be moved back to the hospital under Doctor Martin's care."

"I disagree with that Director. You should allow my people to deal with it."

"I did not ask for your opinion. I was giving you an order Twila."

Twila Allen stood up and stormed out of the room.

Sydney said softly "I have to speak to both of you urgently." She hesitated. "Confidentiality is a priority."

Twila walked back in the room. "The man will be in the hospital in his room in twenty minutes."

"Thank you Twila, you're dismissed." The Director said curtly.

Twila stood for a while. I need to speak to you, Director."

"Make an appointment. Please shut the door."

Twila was stunned as she looked at the Director. She could not believe she was being dismissed. She stepped back walking out of the office shutting the door loudly.

Sydney looked at Ray then the Director. "The man's name is Brian White he was born in 2022. He is a time traveler. There was a project in 2055 called the Genesis Paradox. It was believed to be a theory, it was not." Sydney explained how Brian was moved to the past and jumped to different time periods. She explained the DNA study and the camera recording in his head.

The two men sat shocked at the story. Ray stood up saying "My God can you imagine if that kind of technology was to fall into the wrong hands. A man could be sent back in time and change the future. A rival corporation could have a tremendous advantage."

"The problem is the person would lose their memory like Brian." Sydney said quietly.

"No, I believe with our technology today we could fix that. Or we could send back a message and not a Person."

The Director said quietly, "Doctor Martin I want Rex Bandicardin here with all the information he has. Also you are to gather all the information pertaining to this case and bring it to my office. We will have it secured in a vault in the basement. I do not want anyone to have this information."

Later that morning Bandy followed Sydney into the Director's office. He turned on the computer. The Director, Ray and Sydney sat watching and hearing the past. Bandy had worked on the program so the language could be translated so they could understand. When it was over the information was taken to a secure vault and locked up. No one was to have access without the Director's approval.

Bandy was reinstated to his former position and the others were told to tell no one of the project. Twila Allen was moved to the Chief of Staff position.

Chapter XIX

Brian White would be released from the hospital after many examinations. The small mechanism would be studied extensively. Bandy with other technicians would be able to unravel the mystery. The small machine was capable of creating a small worm hole which enabled Brian to move through time. It was ingenious and complex. The Director had all the plans and prototypes taken to a vault in headquarters to be locked up. His concern was it could be used by a person with no ethics to compromise the past.

Brain was allowed to stay in the company apartments. He was amazed how Governments had been replaced by Corporations. It seemed to be a good system. There were different layers of society and they seemed to get along well. Individuals were allowed to travel to other parts of the country with permission. Should a person be caught spying the penalties were harsh. Long prison sentences with hard labor were enforced. The death penalty was abolished. There were of course some of the same issues with people but for the most part the system worked.

Professors from different Universities talked with Brian. Each of them were told not to reveal who Brian was. To violate this order would result in severe penalties. They were amazed as Brian related his experiences. The Religious scholars were intrigued with John and Mary. Some of the Academic Professors had insisted that the bible was fiction. Mary was a fabrication of a writer. When confronted with Mary they were stunned. The Bible was real. To hear John speak of his time with Jesus was a humbling experience for the skeptics.

Brain often would have dinner with Sydney and her family. He enjoyed their company and would often think of his children when he saw Charlotte and Cory. He felt a deep sadness knowing they were long dead. He would never have the opportunity to meet them.

He met a young Asian girl who was a biochemical engineer. He spent many hours with her as she studied the chip and wiring in his body. They soon became close. He enjoyed being with Myoumi Li. Her ancestry did not include any of his DNA. He wondered if he would jump again into the future. Bandy had told him he had made some adjustments and believed he would not move forward in time. He had found a small algorithm he believed to be the problem.

Myoumi, who was friends with Sydney, told her one evening she was pregnant. She giggled saying "my child will be your grandmother."

Sydney was not sure what to think.

BRIAN SAT IN THE APARTMENT thinking of how much he had experienced. He was happy in the future and wanted to stay. He saw no reason why he needed to return to his time. He would remain in the future for over a year. He would smile as he looked at the small girl who was his daughter. His thoughts would drift back to a time when he held his children he knew were long dead. He wanted to stay and raise his child.

One evening as he lay in bed with Myoumi he felt the familiar pain suddenly shoot through his head. Stepping out of bed holding his head He fell to his knees as the pain became more intense. His body began to shake then he was gone.

Brian opened his eyes in the brightly lit room. He saw a young girl at the side of his bed looking at a computer screen. She looked up and smiled. "You're awake."

She walked to a wall and pressed a button. "He's awake."

In less than a minute two women and two men walked into the room. An attractive woman walked up to him, taking his hand. She placed her other hand on his head and leaned close to him asking "how are you feeling Brian?"

"My head hurts and my back hurts."

"We removed the chip and wiring from your body. I will give you some pain pills for your discomfort." She smiled at him "welcome home."

He watched as the others stared at him. They did not speak.

"Who are you and where am I?"

The woman seemed surprised. "I'm Doctor Wright. Don't you remember me?"

"No, I don't remember anything. I remember waking up on the ground naked. I was in a strange land with strange people. I would leave and wake up in another time and place."

Joanne nodded as she listened. "There must have been a problem with the chip interfering with your memory. What do you remember?"

"I remember from the time I was in a wild country until now, nothing of my past."

"She smiled, "We have been analyzing the data from the chip. We did not intend you to go into the future. We were able to bring you back. You are going to be well soon, We'll let you rest."

Brian was released from the hospital two days later. He still felt pain in his back. He sat with Doctor Wright and spoke of his experience. He was amazed when he was told his DNA was found with Denisovan, Neanthental, and human. The species had mixed and carried his DNA. He had many descendants throughout the world. He was informed that the project had been shut down. It was decided not to keep the project a secret but would share it with a select number of individuals. They would be sworn to secrecy.

When he asked about the future. Joanne said "We are not sure of the impact. We believe it will be minimal."

Bryan and Joanne spent many days together becoming close. They married a year later. He would lay beside her in the dark and wonder of Ela and what she thought of his disappearance. Ivy and her daughter. He saw in research that she had reunited with her husband Dave. They had two boys with her daughter. He wondered as he lay in the dark about Myoumi and her child. He would never meet her. He realized that Myoumi would not have a child since he had returned to the past and he would never meet her. The child would not be born.

He and Joanne would attend church together. He became more spiritual as he read the bible. They would have two girls that would be raised in church. He spent time with the girls watching them grow up. Brian would sometimes watch the information from the chip of his experience. He would see the small pretty dark face of Ela and feel regret knowing she had been left alone. He hoped she would be given a mate. He would see Ivy and her shy and delicate face. He missed them both.

Brian would spend the rest of his life speaking with academics. He found it odd some religious scholars would often disagree with him on John and Mary. They had set opinions and were reluctant to change them. The academic world would gain insight into the life experiences Brian lived.

As an old man he sat in a nursing home as his children, grandchildren, and great grandchildren gathered to celebrate his birthday. He smiled as he looked at a young child named Roberta. She would be Sydney's grandmother.

Chapter XX

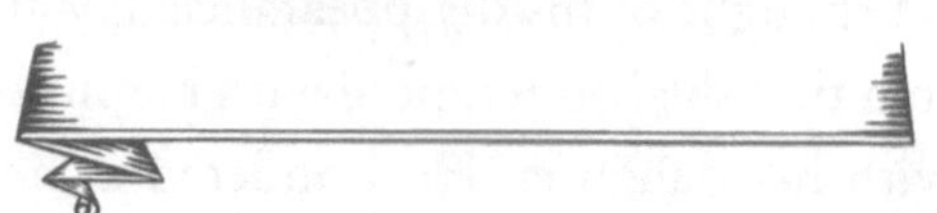

It was raining when Sydney walked into her home. She smiled seeing her family was sitting down to eat. Her daughter jumped up from the table running to her. "Mommy!" The excited girl exclaimed.

Sydney bent down hugging the young girl. "You have not finished your supper Caroline." the robot Simon said, looking at the young girl. She ignored the robot as she walked to the table with her mother. Simon brought out a plate of food. "I saved you a plate, Dr. Martin," he said, sitting a warm plate in front of Sydney."

"Thank you Simon."

As they ate Caroline talked of art class and her teacher. Simon sat feeding Cory, Sydney's son who was one.

"You need to eat your beans." Simon said.

"I only eat beans Grandpa brings me," Carolyn said looking at the plate.

"Jelly beans are not vegetables," Simon said.

"Finish your meal or you won't get dessert." Sydney said smiling.

When they finished supper the family went into the living room. As she sat looking at the drawing Caroline had drawn of a woman on a rock with a tiger on the ground looking up at her the doorbell rang. Simon walked to the door. A messenger robot had arrived with a package.

Simon walked to Sydney and handed it to her. She looked at the old brown paper with her name on it. Simon said "the messenger advised the Americorp main bank has been holding this package for many years. Instructions have been left to deliver it to you on this date."

Sydney was surprised as she looked at the package. Jacob leaned over curiously looking at the package. "Looks like a mystery Syd."

Sydney opened the package seeing an old fashion flash drive. "Now this is strange. I've only seen these in museums." Contemplating the old fashioned flash drive that hadn't been in use for close to a hundred and fifty years. Sydney said "I'll call Bandy, he has a lot of the old computers. I imagine he has something that will play this old flash drive." She called Bandy who arrived half an hour later with an old laptop.

Bandy looked at the old flash drive. "This computer should be able to play the flash drive. It appears to be over a hundred and fifty years old. This is strange, it looks brand new."

The flash drive was inserted into the old laptop computer and soon the old screen flickered on. Sydney, Jacob, Bandy, and Simon sat watching the screen as an older man appeared. He had gray hair and was distinguished looking. He was a nice looking man. The man smiled slightly then he spoke in a soft voice.

"Hello Sydney. You do not remember me but we have met. I am your Grandfather Bryan White. There is a project you have studied called the Genesis Paradox. You and your strange little friend Bandy who I believe is no doubt there with you since he is the only one who has the old machinery that will play this old fashion flash drive. The Genesis Paradox is not a theory but a reality. I traveled back in time where I stayed with Denisovan people for about two years. I traveled forward in time and met John who was a disciple of Jesus and I met Mother Mary. I met and fought with King Richard I, and Napoleon. When I traveled to Guthrie Oklahoma in the 1890's I had a relationship with Ivy Green, she is a Grandmother of yours. I traveled by accident to the future and met you and Bandy. I had a relationship with Myoumi Li and we had a child. When I returned I realized she did not have the child since it was not possible since I returned back to my time."

The man hesitated as the group sat stunned listening to the strange story. Brian continued. "My wife Doctor Joanne Wright White, who was the project director of the Genesis Paradox, has warned me not to contact you. I have decided not to take her advice. I have held your Grandmother Roberta in my arms and felt it is only right to contact you. I have copied the information from my experience onto this flash drive. I had a small camera attached to my octave nerve and it recorded the ten years I was traveling through time. When you see it, you will understand. I do not have the information on how it was done and if I did I would not share it with you. All information concerning the Genesis Paradox has been destroyed. It is too dangerous for human kind. I am sending you this information because I want you to know that life is special and the Lord has a plan for all of us. I know you are a Christian and you will know the story of Jesus is true when you see John and Mary. Please use this information carefully. While I was there the Director had all the information sealed in a vault. You were concerned with an ambitious woman named Twila Allan. Someone like her could use it to benefit herself and do a great deal of damage. When you see the information provided you will understand. Please be careful with his information." The screen went dark.

Sydney was stunned as she watched the video of Brian's experience of traveling through time played out before her on the screen. She could not believe what she was seeing. Bandy fast forward through the scenes then would stop as scenes of different time periods played. They watched the computer for hours. She was shocked as she saw herself as the events unfolded. When it ended she sat quiet.

"It's not possible to time travel. I find it hard to believe but with what we just saw I have to accept, it is possible. He actually came to the future." Sydney stood up, her head was spinning. "We do not know him because he returned to his time. The scientists were able to bring him back to his time, so we would not have remembered him since he was back in his time. Which means he did not come to our time, his future. Which created a paradox. This is unbelievable."

"Sydney you need to be careful who you show this to. I think it could be dangerous if it fell into the wrong hands. Someone like Twila Allen could exploit it." Jacob said, walking up to his wife taking her hand.

"I agree," she said. She looked at Bandy, "not a word Bandy, do not tell anyone of this."

"Who would believe it? I'm banished in the depths of a basement. Who would listen to me?"

The following days Sydney verified the information on the flashdrive. She was stunned seeing the family tree of Brian White. It was exactly as the information he provided. She saw the extensive work of Dr. Joanne Wright; there was no information in her work from 2055 to 2065. She found where Joanne Wright married Brian and had two daughters. One of them was a Grandmother of Twila Allen. She was shocked to be related to her.

Ray Turner sat quietly in his chair as he listened to Sydney. He did not speak as he watched the video of Brian's life while he was traveling through time. When it finished he took a deep breath. "We need to be careful with this information. I will need to speak to the Director. I am concerned that if an unethical person were to have this information they could use it to benefit themselves and damage the future."

"Someone like Twila Allen." Sydney said just above a whisper.

Ray frowned, "Yes, someone exactly like her." Ray stood up "I will speak to the Director tomorrow morning. He will want to see the video."

Sydney stood up "Ray would you consider bringing Bandy back to Headquarters? He is talented." She held her breath.

"Ray smiled, "yes I will have Bandy reinstated tomorrow." He stopped at the door, turning to look at Sydney. "My wife will be happy. Bandy is her nephew."

The Director did share the information with a select group of people they were sworn to secrecy and were told if information was to leak out they would pay a heavy penalty. He also made it clear the Genesis Paradox was not to be recreated. It was too dangerous and the consequences were too great to take a chance on.

Chapter XXI

Derrick Calvey took a deep breath then rang the doorbell. When the door opened he took a sharp intake of breath. He saw Twila Allen standing in the doorway. She was wearing black silk pajamas, with a red silk robe robe trimmed in black. Her long red hair falling over her shoulders made her look like a vision. She was beautiful.

Twila stood with her hand on the door looking at Derrick. She frowned as her forehead wrinkled. "Is there something you want Derrick. Why are you disturbing me at home?"

Derrick looked away from the slender body of Twila as his face went a slight red. He stammered as he spoke. "I, well I don't mean to bother you at home, but I have information you will want to have."

She did not smile. "It couldn't wait until tomorrow when I'm in the office?"

Derrick looked directly into her eyes. "No, I assure you Twila this is something you will want to see in private."

Twila stood for a short time contemplating what Derrick said. She knew Derrick well. He was in research and development, and was ambitious. Derrick was also unethical, and greedy. He had been implicated in a controversy when Asians were caught trying to leave Americorp land. They had been caught at the Boston harbor with sensitive information. They were arrested and found guilty of espionage. They named several people in the scheme. Derrick was not identified but was suspected. Consequently he was removed from his position and reassigned. Twila had agreed to take him in Research and

Development. He was bright and worked hard and had been involved in many advances with computers.

Twila stepped back saying "come in Derrick."

Derrick smiled and walked past Twila. He was impressed with the lavish home.

The living room was decorated with modern furniture. He walked to a desk and sat his computer down.

He said "I have a friend at the University that has information that we were visited by a time traveler. My friend says the Professor she works for has seen information on the man. It was called the Genesis Paradox. We of course do not remember the man because he returned to his own time. Since he returned to his time we could not possibly know him because he did not return." Derrick smiled at Twila. "That is why it is a Paradox."

Twila did not smile. "I have been hearing the same rumors at Headquarters. If it were true the Director would have told me. I am a Deputy Director."

Derrick hesitated choosing his words carefully. "Twila I don't believe the Director trusts you. I'm hearing you will be replaced."

The anger flashed in Twila's eyes. "That is not true!"

Derrick turned on the computer. He said softly. "You know it is true Twila because you are a threat to the old man and the other Deputy Directors. Everyone knows that Ray Turner is next in line to take over as Director. You are sharper and should be the next Director, but you're not going to be because of politics."

Twila was quiet; she knew she was being shut out of meetings and information that was being given to other Deputy Directors was not shared with her. She knew Ray was an enemy who was advising the Director to remove her. "So why are you here?"

Derrick's smile grew. "This is why." he said as he stepped back from the computer. "The Genesis Paradox has been solved by our researchers. You are aware it has always been considered a theory. It is possible to travel through time. I realize the Director has ordered it stopped but we have cracked it. We can go back into time and make changes we want and change the future. Our future."

Twila watched the computer and was stunned seeing the evidence presented and realized it was true. When the presentation was over she walked to her couch sitting down. She thought of how she could make this work for her. She looked up and smiled at Derrick. Her eyes grew soft as her beauty was highlighted. She sat back and with a seductive look asked, "Who all knows about this Derrick?"

Derrick stared at the beautiful woman and was mesmerized. "Only a few, Me, and well three others, Melinda, Gary, and James."

Twila stood up walking to Derrick. "Good," she said, taking his hand standing close to him. "I want this quiet. Come to my office and we will discuss it."

"Alright, I will and I know the others will not say anything." His heart was beating fast as he breathed heavily standing so close to Twila. She reached up, placing her small hand on his cheek. She stepped closer and kissed his cheek. Her green eyes looked directly into his dark eyes.

"You were right to bring this to me. Together we will change things for our future." She hesitated as she looked into Derrick's eyes. He was stunned as he saw the beautiful woman in front of him. He reached out putting his arms around her waist. She stepped back smiling. "I'll see you in the morning Derrick."

Derrick walked out of the house, his head spinning.

Twila walked into her office the following morning. She saw Alice Covenington sitting and talking to her assistant. Alice stood up as Twila shut the door behind her.

"I have the numbers you were asking for." Alice said not smiling. She had stayed late to correlate the information. She knew Twila had given her a short deadline since she did not like her. She also knew Twila was making a point with her. Alice had expected to be the Deputy Director, but the Director had chosen Twila, who was ruthless and made life difficult for all her employees. Alice smiled, "I believe you will be pleased with the numbers this quarter."

Twila smiled, taking the papers. "Thank you Alice." She walked into her office, shutting the door behind her.

Derrick walked into Twilas office sitting across the large desk. Twila leaned forward "I've been thinking we need to send a robot back in time that has been programmed with specific information. We only need to go back say ten years. The robot will be fitted to look like the ones available for that time period."

"I agree," Derrick said thinking of the possibilities. "We can fit the robot with the wiring it will take to create a black hole. He should not be affected by the stress of traveling through a black hole. Do you have a time you are looking at for the robot to go back into?"

"Yes I do." Twila said, sitting back smiling broadly.

Chapter XXII

The robot stood up looking around. It had been programmed to head for the Americorp headquarters and inject data into the mainframe. No one would suspect the robot since it would be disguised as a maintenance robot. The plan was simple, the robot would arrive ten years into the past. Twila would be promoted on that date to Chief of Staff where she would be in charge of all daily operations. It was a powerful position and she would be the youngest person to hold that position. She would be promoted seven years later to Deputy Director. Information would over time be sent to her computer. The Robot would also make contact with Twila with specific instructions it would give to her.

The robot had arrived sixteen years into the past, rather than ten. It would follow its programming and head for the Headquarters of Americorp. As the robot walked on the wide sidewalk traffic was heavy for the day. The hover vehicles moved smoothly along carrying people to their designated work areas. The Robot was intelligent with the most sophisticated artificial intelligence embedded into its hardware. It however was a machine and had a specific mission. The fact that it had been sent to the wrong period of time did not occur to the machine that its mission would be compromised. The Robot continued on its mission.

Twila Allen was excited to be working as an intern in the Americorp headquarters. She was finishing her last year at the University and had landed a position in the Headquarters building.

It was the most important intern position which many of the other students had wanted. She had worked hard and her efforts had paid off. Now she was an intern for Research and Development in Headquarters. She worked with the other technicians who were helpful and took time to explain the operations. She was truly happy knowing she would graduate in the spring and marry Kelvin her finance. He was studying theology, his plan was to be a missionary. She had lost her Mother at a young age and had recently lost her Father. It had been a test of her faith but Kelvin was there to help her through the sad time of losing her Father. She smiled thinking how he had helped her keep her faith. Without him she would have felt hopeless. She loved him more than anything.

The Robot saw in the distance a large crane lifting a heavy I-beam. The crane was computerized, which ensured the beam was placed in perfect position high in the air as other robots welded it in place. When the Robot was drawing near to the construction site a gust of wind caught the I-beam that was high into the air. It began to whip wildly in the wind. The heavy cables snapped as the I-beam fell. All robots were programmed to protect humans. The robot reacted quickly seeing the falling beam.

A hoover vehicle with passengers was moving quickly down the street. The Robot seeing the falling I-beam raced for the vehicle. Reaching the hover vehicle the robot pushed the front of it causing the hover vehicle to move sharply away from the falling I-beam as it fell crashing to the ground. It narrowly missed the vehicle. The robot was hit by the I-beam being crushed.

Passengers exited the crashed vehicle seeing the huge I-beam and the crushed robot. Suddenly a small explosion was heard. Kelvin Bryant who was sitting at the front of the hover vehicle walked to the robot seeing it had self-destructed. He found it odd since only military robots were equipped with self destruct mechanisms. He had served his two years mandatory service in military service working on robots programmed for battle. He stared at the odd machine realizing it was sophisticated. When security services arrived he pointed out the strange machine and explained how it self-destructed. The security forces picked it up and removed it. The machine would be taken to Security operations. Very little information would be gained since the robot had self-destructed, destroying any evidence it carried. It would be an unsolved mystery for years.

Kelvin stepped back looking at the hover machine. He said a silent prayer of thanks knowing if the robot had not moved the hover vehicle the passengers would be dead. He was thankful to be alive.

Twila smiled brightly at Kelvin seeing him at a table of their favorite restaurant. He was sitting on the patio which she preferred.

Kelvin stood up kissing her cheek. He told Twila of the accident and how close to dying he had come. Her eyes filled with tears saying softly "I don't know what I would do if something happened to you since all I have in the world is you."

Kelvin smiled at her, taking her hand. "No, honey the Lord is always with You, have faith."

Twila wiped her eyes and talked of working at Americorp. She liked the job and was learning so much from the technicians.

"Do you want to stay with Americorp? I'm sure you would do well there." Kelvin asked as he watched Twila.

"Oh I don't know. I think I would prefer to go with you as you tramp around the world preaching the gospel."

"I was hoping you would say that. I was worried you would like corporate life.

Twila opened her eyes hearing a noise. She looked at her husband Kelvin sleeping beside her. She smiled watching him. He had been a missionary for sixteen years. He had accepted a position as Minister at a church in Chicago when their daughter Sabrina was six. Sabrina had been born in Saint Petersburg. Both Kelvin and Twila decided to move home before she started school. They had decided to settle down in Chicago and raise their family. When their second daughter came along two years later both were happy to not be traveling.

Twila stepped out of bed putting on her cotton robe. She walked into the kitchen seeing her two daughters standing on chairs at the oven.

"What are you two up too?"

The two girls grinned, "we're making breakfast for you and Daddy!"

Twila smiled as she looked at the goo in the pot.

"I don't believe you or Kelvin will want to eat this Twila." Peter the Robot said passively.

"No, it's good, it really is," Linda, her youngest daughter protested.

Twila walked to the table sitting down. Kelvin walked in looking at the two young girls at the stove. He sat across from Twila.

She smiled, "your girls are preparing breakfast."

The two girls brought over a plate of what looked like slime placing a plate in front of their parents. Kelvin with a spoon dipped it in the slime and took a bite. It was so sweet he almost gagged. "This is good," he said while taking a drink of water.

Twila also tasted the food. She smiled, "It is good."

"I don't recommend you eat that" Peter said "the sugar and calorie content is extremely high."

When the breakfast was finished with only a few bites Kelvin asked "Are you going on a field trip today Linda?"

"Yes, we're going to the jungle and we'll see lions and tigers."

Twila laughed, "we're going to the wildlife refuge where there are large trees and different animals. I don't believe there will be tigers."

The two girls went to their rooms to get ready for school. Peter brought them a biscuit with egg and cheese.

"I believe this will be more nutritious." He picked up the plate of slime taking them to the sink.

"I had that strange dream again last night," Twila said as she ate her biscuit.

"What dream?" Kelvin asked.

"I was at your funeral." she hesitated as the emotions flowed over her. "I was in an office and was so angry. I was not a nice person." she looked down as she thought of the recurring dream she had often."

She felt Kelvin's hand on hers. "It was a dream, that's all. You have an active imagination."

"It seemed so real. I don't know what would have happened if..." Her words trailed off.

"I didn't die in the accident. You need to stop worrying. The Lord was with me and is with you."

"I know," she said quietly.

Twila, Sabrina, and Linda arrived at the school. She kissed Sabrina goodbye watching as she ran to the large building with other children going inside. She took Linda's hand and walked to the large hoover bus. Inside Linda sat next to Caroline. Twila sat next to Sydney. "Good morning Doctor Martin."

"Good morning Twila, are you ready for the adventure?"

"Yes I'm sure it will be fun going to the wildlife refuge with twenty-five, four and five year olds."

Riding the bus Carolyn explained the picture to her friend Linda.

"This is mommy on the rock, and the tiger is mean. His name is Simon."

"The tiger's name is not Simon and I have explained that it is not appropriate." Simon said passively.

Twila turned in her seat looking at the picture. "That is a pretty picture Carolyn."

"Yes it is of a woman who lived in a cave. The Tiger is trying to eat her."

"What happened to the woman from the cave?"

Carolyn thought for a while then said "She jumps on the tigers back and rides it home. She tells Simon to stop being naughty and he is nice and stops eating people."

"That is not appropriate. I believe Carolyn's imagination is out of control Doctor Martin."

Sydney giggled. "It will be okay Simon. I will talk with her later."

The bus arrived at the wildlife refuge where the children saw different animals roaming freely in open fields. They were kept inside by a forcefield. The children walked through the trees on trails seeing rabbits and squirrels. They would return home with an adventure to tell.

That evening as Sydney sat in the living room alone. She was lost in her thoughts thinking of the strange story she had heard earlier that week. A messenger robot had arrived delivering an old flash drive. Her friend Bandy had brought over his older laptop computer and when she, her husband Jacob, and Bandy watched the story unfold Brian White had told, it shocked all of them. Seeing the past unfold before her eyes was amazing. Most shocking was the scene of her with Brian White, who was her Grandfather from a hundred years ago. Her Grandmother, Ivy Green was from three hundred years in the past. The future had changed. It was a paradox of time and choice. Sydney realized without Brian traveling back in time, Jacob, whose ancestor was a Denisovan woman, Ela would not have become pregnant. Jacob would not have been born. Her Grandmother Ivy Green would not have been pregnant with Brian's child, She would not have been born. Their children would not have been born. Brian's

time travel and choices changed the future.

"Is everything alright Doctor Martin?" Simon asked.

"Yes, Simon, I was thinking of the information from the old flash drive we saw earlier this week with my Grandfather Brian White. It was so strange to see myself interacting with him, knowing that it was a different future. I do not remember him since he returned to his own time which changed our future. It of course is a paradox because events of that future and choices have changed our present time since he remained in his time, and died there in his time, not able to be a part of our current future." She rubbed her head. "It gives me a headache trying to wrap my mind around how the future is now different. I wonder about his concern about Twila Allen. She has never worked for Americorp except as an intern years ago. Twila is our minister's wife, and one of the kindest people I have ever met. There must be another Twila Allen." Sydney sat quietly contemplating the strange story and all the possibilities.

"I would like to have met him." She said after a short time. "I have seen pictures of him in old photo albums, he was handsome. I still wonder how it could be possible that he traveled to our time. It just doesn't seem possible. All information concerning the genesis paradox has been removed and locked in a vault. The Director feels it is too dangerous a technology."

According to Albert Einstein it is possible. Should his theories be correct as many Physicists believe they are, then traveling through time is possible with the right technology. Brian White's traveling across time created a paradox in time which means the past would have changed which in turn affected our future." Simon said passively.

"I wonder how our world has changed because of his arrival. Was it for the best or is the future worse because of it." Sydney asked, still deep in thought.

"I suppose it would depend on your perspective." Simon said, "you will of course not know because your future is your reality."

Sydney smiled. "You are right Simon. I'm going to believe the future is bright and it is a better place because of my Grandpa Brian White.

the end

Don't miss out!

Visit the website below and you can sign up to receive emails whenever RB Parkline publishes a new book. There's no charge and no obligation.

https://books2read.com/r/B-A-PNYC-ZXUYC

BOOKS2READ

Connecting independent readers to independent writers.